Tales of the Grotesque:
A Collection of Uneasy Tales

Tales of the Grotesque:
A Collection of Uneasy Tales

L. A. Lewis

Shadow Publishing

TALES OF THE GROTESQUE:
A COLLECTION OF UNEASY TALES

SECOND EDITION 2017

ISBN: 978-0-9572962-0-6

Shadow Publishing
Apt 19 Awdry Court
15 St Nicolas Gardens
Kings Norton
Birmingham
B38 8BH
UK
david.sutton986@btinternet.com

Dedicated to the memory
of
Elizabeth Yeardye Lewis

Contents

The Quest for Lewis

By Richard Dalby

I FIRST HEARD about the *Creeps* series during the twelve months of my first job, working in the London office of Harper & Row at 69 Great Russell Street, a hundred yards from the British Museum.

We often received mail for Philip Allan *&* Co. Ltd., but no one knew anything about this company, and there was no forwarding address. They had apparently moved away in the early days of the war. None of my colleagues at Harpers realised that Philip Allan himself was still alive and active, and living in Bishop's Stortford, serving as Editor-in-chief of *The Journal of Criminal Law* which he had founded in 1937 and continued to run until his death in 1973 aged 89.

Already an aficionado of M. R. James, E. F. Benson, and Cynthia Asquith's *Ghost Books*, I gradually began to discover and acquire secondhand (usually very worn) copies of the *Creeps* for a few pence each.

It gave me much satisfaction to know that I was working in the very same rooms where the three Allan directors—Philip Allan, A.D. Marks, and C. L. Birkin—worked in the 1930s, and where so many anthologies and collections of ghost and horror stories, including *They Return at Evening* by H. Russell Wakefield and *Who Wants a Green Bottle?* by Tod Robbins, plus several non-fiction titles by Elliott O'Donnell and the fascinating *Oddities* and *Enigmas* by Rupert T Gould, had come to fruition in the past.

The selection of stories in the *Creeps* series was very 'curate's-eggish', with a few excellent gems secreted among the dross.

But one title stood head and shoulders above the rest—a truly

1

memorable and original collection, *Tales of the Grotesque*, by a completely unknown author, L. A. Lewis. Unlike so many stories in the genre which soon fade from the mind, these ten stories were truly unforgettable.

I soon found one more solitary story by Lewis, namely 'The Author's Tale', in Christine Campbell Thomson's anthology *Terror by Night* (1935), reprinted in *The 'Not at Night' Omnibus* (1937), but could discover no more. I wrote to both C.C. Thomson and Sir Charles (Lloyd) Birkin, enquiring about L.A. Lewis, but they could tell me nothing, beyond surmising that he/she was a male author. Further lines of enquiry proved equally fruitless.

Eventually, thirty years ago, I unexpectedly made direct contact with Lewis's widow through a newspaper advertisement. She had no remaining copies of her husband's *Tales of the Grotesque*, and I was able to give her a recently acquired spare copy.

Following a short correspondence, I went to visit her at the Manor House, Hingham, near Wymondham in Norfolk, where she lived in one of the flats designed for senior citizens. She was very sprightly and amiable, looking younger than her 85 years.

As no biographical details of any kind had ever appeared in print, I naturally tried to learn all I could about the mysterious L.A. Lewis. Initially she was very guarded with personal details about her husband, but I quickly realised he had suffered much tragedy and mental anguish (with brief references to padded cells and suicide attempts) throughout his life.

By degrees, however, I was eventually able to piece together the basic details of his life (with additional confirmation at the Registry of Births & Deaths at St. Catherine's House in London).

Leslie Allin Lewis was born on 6th February 1899 at 94 Ruston Road in Sheffield, and raised on the family estate at East Hendred in

Berkshire. He was an enthusiastic writer from early childhood, and several of his stories and articles appeared in ephemeral, long-forgotten magazines. During his schooldays (at Royce's, in Abingdon) he wrote—and had bound into three volumes—a series of stories about "Blackie", a fantasy panther. He also illustrated these tales, being a talented artist in his youth.

In 1916 Lewis joined the Artist's Rifles and was later commissioned in the Royal Flying Corps, training at Hendon to become a pilot (alongside John Metcalfe, another budding master of macabre fiction). In April 1917 he went to France, remaining on active service there for a year and flying Sopwith Camels. After the war Flight-Lieutenant Lewis took a course in Aero Engineering, and also obtained his 'A' and 'B' Licences as a pilot. Later he took his instructor's licence. For a short period he was engaged in Circus Flying.

His long experience as a Squadron-Leader, and his belief that aeroplanes had souls, resulted in some of his most memorable stories, notably 'Haunted Air' and 'The Iron Swine'. The latter was based on a Junker aeroplane which Lewis took to Germany for a friend, as all German machines required a Certificate of Airworthiness in Germany as well as in Britain.

'Animate in Death' was written after a pike fishing expedition to the Norfolk Broads. He greatly enjoyed angling and boating.

Many autobiographical touches can be found in all these stories, especially 'The Tower of Moab' where an ex-pilot's vision of a whole galaxy of unearthly creatures and ghosts spanning the space between heaven and hell leads to terrifying consequences.

Lewis never doubted the existence of demonic creatures and elementals on the other side of the 'web' which divides the astral from the physical. Some of these monstrous gremlins and evilly alluring entities, which continually strive to break through into our

3

world, are graphically described in this book—almost as if the author genuinely thought he had witnessed these sights, rather than their merely stemming from an active imagination.

Mrs. Lewis confirmed that her husband had suffered from 'hallucinations', and these became worse as the years passed. She told me that 'The Tower of Moab' was based on a real tower which was being built by an American religious sect, but never finished, at the time Lewis first saw it, supposedly somewhere in South London.

Some of his stories, including 'The Chords of Chaos', originally appeared in magazines published by the Theosophical Society, but it was not until September 1934 that his ten *Tales of the Grotesque* were collected together in Philip Allan's *Creeps* series. Curiously, the book was never published in the U.S.A., then enjoying a boom in supernatural and macabre literature, the golden period of *Weird Tales*—Lewis's tales would surely have appealed to readers of that magazine.

Lewis wrote several more stories in the late 1930s and early 1940s, but none of these were ever accepted for publication. They may have been far more horrific and 'grotesque' than his earlier tales. We will never know for sure. After he was invalided out of the RAF in the early 1940s, facing permanent unemployment, he destroyed all his remaining work during a fit of manic depression.

His later years were much blighted by deteriorating physical and mental health, but he found solace with his longtime friend Elizabeth Yeardye Rickell. In the late 1940s they lived in Lowestoft, before marrying and settling in their final home at Ealing. After succumbing to blindness and myocardial degeneration, he died from a heart attack in St. Bernard's Hospital, Southall, on 28th October 1961, aged 62.

Elizabeth Lewis had already given her only remaining photograph of Leslie to the RAF Museum at Hendon by the time I first met her, and no manuscripts (not even 'Blackie') or letters had been preserved.

She was completely unaware that any of his stories had ever been reprinted since the war in anthologies (which by then were out-of-print). Knowing my interest in reprinting her husband's complete tales, she thoughtfully bequeathed his literary copyrights to me on her death in 1988.

Leslie Allin Lewis undoubtedly earns a high place among the best masters of supernatural and macabre literature that Britain has ever produced. With the addition of 'The Author's Tale', the present collection represents the first complete edition of the unique and stunning *Tales of the Grotesque*. This complete edition was first published by the Ghost Story Press in 1994 and 2003, both times in a strictly limited hardback format; and now makes its debut as a paperback, eighty years after the original *Creeps* edition.

LOST KEEP

PETER HUNT was barely seventeen when news reached him of his Aunt Kate's death in a North London hospital, and, knowing that she was almost penniless, he entertained no expectation of benefits as her only surviving relative. It was with some surprise, therefore, that he read in the Matron's letter of the despatch of a small, locked box, recently brought from a safe-deposit to her bed-side, to which she had evidently attached great importance. By the same post there also arrived a package from his Aunt herself addressed in the weak, spidery calligraphy of extreme age, enclosing a key and a brief note which read: 'To my nephew, Peter Hunt. Open the box and make what use Fate wills of its contents.'

The box arrived by delivery van in the evening of the same day, and was carried upstairs by Peter himself to his mean back bedroom in a Tilbury lodging-house. It was not very heavy, and any hope of hoarded coin vanished as soon as he lifted it, though there remained, of course, the slender chance of banknotes or bearer bonds. He cut the cords with which its lock had been reinforced and, taking the key from his pocket, opened it. It contained three objects only: a small-scale model of a stone fortress mounted on a pedestal shaped to resemble a rocky hill, a folded sheet of paper, and something which looked like a silver-framed magnifying glass, except that its lens was opaque—almost black, in fact—and nearly impervious to light.

Peter drew the miniature towards him—it was no more than three inches high—and examined it as closely as the poor light from the dirty window would allow. It was too early to use the gas. The meter was always ravenous for his pennies.

Even to his untutored eyes the workmanship of the model was exquisite, the degree of finish seeming to represent a lifetime's labour.

Every single stone block—and there were thousands—in the structure of the building had been faithfully reproduced, and even such detail as patches of lichen had not been overlooked. With luck the thing should be worth several pounds as a curiosity. Perhaps he would have it valued by Christie's; it wouldn't do to trust 'Uncle' Abe at the corner shop. He pushed it aside and reached for the folded paper, recognising his father's characteristic handwriting as he smoothed it out. It related to the contents of the box, and read as follows—

'I, Vernon John Hunt, having been given by the doctors three months to live, have determined to put in writing what is known of "Lost Keep", of which this scale model has been handed down from parent to child for many generations.

'Tradition has it that the miniature was made under pain of death by an Italian craftsman condemned by an early ancestor to imprisonment in the original stronghold until such time as he should complete the task. That he *did* complete it the miniature itself testifies, but history does not relate whether his release followed or whether, with the callousness of feudal days, he was left to rot in his prison. There is, I regret to say, some ground for the latter supposition, for he is credited in the Latin manuscript, now destroyed, with having laid some kind of curse on this piece of craftsmanship. A peculiarity of the whole matter is that there have been so many female heirs that the name of the original title-holders is forgotten, the heirloom having passed haphazard from male to female issue and so transferred itself to various different families. Even the locality of the original site is unrecorded—hence its name of "Lost Keep"—and the curse of the modeller is concerned with this fact. The fortress, if it still stands, may be in Iceland, Scandinavia, Russia, or, for that matter, any part of the world; but, translating from the Latin script, it is supposed to be rediscoverable by anyone who has *"the wit or fortune to combine glass and facsimile with understanding."* Whoever solves the riddle, however, is threatened with *"greater temptations of the Devil than have beset any other of Adam's descendants,"* and, if he succumbs, will find *"death in the home at the hand of his son."* Doubtless each successive holder of the heirloom has attacked the problem, though there is no rumoured instance of its solution. I in my turn have wasted hours in speculation as to the purpose of the dark glass, shaped so like a lens, yet so obviously useless as such, and have examined every point of the model's surface with a normal reading-glass for signs of engraved lettering, but have learned no more than to marvel at the delicacy of the work. On the latter count the model would probably be of considerable value among collectors, but its secret, if it really possesses one, is well hidden.

'So, being under *sentence* of death, I entrust this sole heirloom of a family whose fortunes are at ebb to my sister *Kate*, requesting her to hold it for my son Peter until her death or his majority.'

The document was neither dated nor signed.

Peter leaned back and looked, with a distaste that familiarity had never conquered, round the shabby room. So his father had believed the model to be of value too? So much the better. He'd have no false sentiment about parting with it since he'd never even heard of it till today, and he'd certainly get it valued at an early opportunity. It ought to fetch enough to pay for a course of night classes at a technical school, or—with great luck—a real college career, for which he could drop his present job as warehouse packer and fit himself to enter those higher spheres that his hereditary instinct craved. Meanwhile, his day's work was finished and he could not afford to go out looking for amusement. He might as well have a shot at the dark glass problem.

Picking the apparently useless thing up, he studied it closely. It certainly *looked* like a lens, being a circle of some vitreous composition thick at the centre, thin at the sides, and mounted in a metal ring. Lighting the gas-jet—an old-fashioned fish-tail burner—he held the thing to the light, but through its opacity could distinguish only a shapeless blurr. Perhaps distance, either from the eyes or the object to be focused, would sharpen its outline. He experimented thus, standing at arm's length from the jet, and gradually advancing the glass towards the flame. At really close quarters it *did* seem to let through a little more light, and he was so occupied with this discovery that he never thought of the effect which the accompanying heat might have on the glass until a sharp snap followed by a tinkle on the

10

linoleum informed him that he had cracked it.

With a muttered expletive the boy turned it over, and at once noticed an interesting fact. The glass appeared to be built up in layers, and the heat had split off a piece of the outer one, revealing a second and seemingly undamaged surface beneath.

He pursed his lips in a whistle. The discovery might have some bearing on the apparent uselessness of the object. It was a natural conclusion that a perfect lens might be hidden under the dark covering, though the purpose of all the secrecy and mystery woven around glass and miniature was more than Peter could guess. He found his pen-knife and, carefully inserting it under the broken edge, split off another fragment. Once started, the remainder came away so easily that in a few minutes he had completely exposed the underlying surface, the layer on the other side flaking away with equal facility after a light rap with the handle of the knife. The now transparent lens—tinted, as far as he could judge against the twilight with his back to the gas, a kind of smoky blue—possessed an astounding power of magnification when he tried it on the back of his hand. The hand, as such, in fact, completely disappeared, and the circle of glass showed only a portion of the skin enlarged to a degree which he would have thought only a microscope could achieve. As he watched, the enlarging process seemed to continue as though concentric rings of the tissue were rolling out from the centre and vanishing through the rim. He had a sickening sensation of being about to sink bodily into the glass, and, hastily shutting his eyes, put it down on the table. The queer sensation passed off rapidly, but left him with a mixed feeling of giddiness, excitement, and fear. There was something *uncanny* about the lens—*damned* uncanny—but his faults did not include cowardice, and he resolved to complete his experiments single-handed. With this decision he proceeded to lock the door and, pulling the table as near as he could to the gas-jet, sat down to test the effect of the lens on the miniature.

The grey, perpetual twilight had neither brightened nor darkened by one iota when Peter completed his seventh circuit of the mighty battlements. Dizzily far below him the waves of an apparently tideless sea broke and hissed back along the same bank of shingle, neither advancing nor retiring, each followed by an interminable succession of troughs and crests sweeping in from a vague horizon that seemed infinitely distant from the high eminence upon which he stood. But for their maddeningly regular beat no sound whatever broke the silence, no breeze moved the cold and stagnant air, and throughout the gigantic mass of masonry he was the only thing that lived. Above him the sky was a leaden monotony, broken at one place alone by a mere pin-point of light which appeared to be a far-off beacon. It shone where the diminishing thread of a titanic causeway merged into the sky-line.

Peter drew a clammy hand across his eyes and leaned wearily against the ramparts. Was he *mad?* Or had some unbelievable miracle literally transported him in a flash of time from his dingy back-room to this far-distant and eerie place? That he was not dreaming his sore knuckles proved, where he had struck them hard against unyielding stone in the panic frenzy of his incredible translation. He said aloud, 'O God!' in a meaningless sort of way, and repeated it several times, partly for the love of any sound other than that of the waves, and partly to focus his attention. Though he could not then have put it into words, the panorama, to his rather limited mind accustomed to concrete surroundings, savoured alarmingly of the Abstract.

Resolutely directing his gaze at the nearest buttress of the ramparts, he went over in his mind, perhaps for the twentieth time, the series of his sensations from the moment when he had held the lens over the model. Through the glass the tiny castle had appeared to grow and grow in swiftly overlapping rings from its centre, there had been a feeling of suction as though he were being dragged violently towards it, and then a moment—or an hour—of complete black-out from which he had emerged to a realisation of standing in an immense copy of the miniature courtyard looking up at the terrific mass of the Keep. Appalled by its sickening height and crushed by his own proportional sense of smallness, he had nevertheless been impelled to enter the open door and climb endlessly up flight after flight of stone steps till he came out, weak and trembling, on the roof. And then the feverish pacing of its periphery, a prey to wonder, fear, and a horrible giddiness each time he looked down towards the sea. And all the time the grey, unnatural twilight had persisted, torment-ing him with the half-knowledge that he was not even on the Earth at all, but in some incredible place utterly divorced from all things human and alive.

It was healthy, physical hunger that eventually restored his mental balance to something near normality. In whatever nightmare realm he had landed himself, it clearly contained no possible source of food, and he must find his way out before starvation overtook him. The castle was sea-girt, and the interminable causeway that stretched from the shore towards the horizon was the only apparent means of exit. He felt a trifle fortified at the prospect of escape, and eagerly began the long descent of the stairways.

'The glass,' Mrs. Stebbings repeated defiantly, 'ain't here, and I ain't took it. Them bits in the 'earth might be it—broke—but that don't tell me where young 'Unt 'as 'opped orf to.' She tossed her head. 'And 'im owing me a week's rent,' she added with meaning.

13

The Police Sergeant turned from his inspection of the broken lock and gave her an expressionless glance. 'That's all right,' he replied, 'I'm not accusing you of taking it, but it certainly isn't in this room. No doubt Hunt has it with him—that's to say if there *is* a glass, as this writing states.

'Now, Mrs. S.,' he went on pacifically, 'please see if your other lodger is in the house. We shall want him to confirm your account of breaking into this room—not that we doubt your word,' he added hastily, 'just as a matter of form.' As the landlady's footsteps died away on the rickety stairs he turned to the Constable who accompanied him.

'Another mare's nest, I fancy,' he remarked. 'Lodger owes week's rent and can't pay, so leaves quietly. Can't smuggle his stuff out 'cause she's too sharp-eyed. Clothes aren't worth much, anyway. Hard on the lady, of course, but scarcely one of the cases where we call in the Yard.' He paused, and looked thoughtfully around him. 'All the same,' he continued, 'it *is* a bit queer how he got out with the door locked inside. The window's too big a drop, the roof's out of reach, and there are no marks on the key to show he turned it from outside with forceps.'

'How long's he been missing?' asked the Constable.

The Sergeant consulted his watch. 'About forty-two hours. She saw him coming upstairs with a parcel—probably this,' he indicated the box and model on the table, 'about five p.m. on Saturday, left him to sleep, as she supposed, all yesterday, and got the other fellow to break the lock when he didn't come down to breakfast this morning, and she found the door fastened. Yes, it looks like a case of convenient disappearance, seeing that he's not turned up at his job. Well, she ought to get her rent and a bit over on the price of this miniature if he doesn't come back to claim it after a reasonable interval. But I doubt if she'll see Master Hunt again in *this* house,' he concluded.

'For God's sake water—and food,' said a hoarse, feeble voice behind them, and they swung round in amazement to see the missing lodger, pale and haggard, sprawled across the bed!

That familiarity breeds contempt is a proverb of some antiquity and more than a little justification, and, although contempt was the last sentiment Peter Hunt felt with regard to Lost Keep, it was not long before his initial fear of the unknown was transmuted into a complacent acceptance of his heritage and of the supernatural powers it conveyed. His circumstances at the age of thirty differed vastly from those in which the arrival of the remarkable miniature had found him. He now possessed a house in Park Lane, a country-seat down in Dorset, three cars, a large staff of servants for the upkeep of his establishments, and, above all, a very charming but neglected wife among whose many contributions to his well-being was a son and heir also named Peter, but generally known as Pete for purposes of distinction.

It was in the library of his Park Lane mansion that Peter was sitting one August evening when a telephone call informed him that Lord Knifton proposed calling on him for a private interview in half an hour's time, and Peter's thin lips twisted into a grimace of satisfaction as he hung up the receiver. Knifton was his co-director in many of the big commercial enterprises from which his income was derived, and he had lately been behaving in a most obstructive way by refusing to approve certain conversion schemes which he—Peter—had evolved for their joint enrichment at the expense of the shareholders. He was one of the few financial magnates sufficiently powerful to interfere seriously with Peter's activities, and the time had come when one or the other must definitely take second place.

Well, Knifton might indulge in whatever ideals he chose, but Peter *knew* which of them that one would be.

He opened the drawer of his desk and took out the miniature fortress. The hard circle of the lens pressed comfortingly against his abdomen in the inner pocket where it always reposed. A thousand Kniftons could not dominate the master of Lost Keep.

With half an hour's leisure, Peter's thoughts wandered back to the day when he had discovered the trick of the model and so nearly lost his life in the discovery. Even now he shuddered to recall that unending march along the rocky causeway that seemed to lead on eternally towards an horizon that never grew a mile nearer. How that unchanging grey twilight had mocked him with its denial of Time after he had dropped his watch into the sea and had no means of counting the passage of the hours. The sullen waves had lapped on with changeless rhythm either side of him, raising and lowering their fringe of decaying weed with never a variation in the limit of their lift—until he had screamed aloud at their inexorable monotony. He remembered how he had tramped on, mile after mile, towards the ever-receding sky-line till sheer exhaustion had dropped him in his tracks, and how, as he fell, his hand doubled under him, had come in contact with the lens which he then recollected having slipped into his pocket just as unconsciousness was claiming him in the Tilbury bedroom. With tired fingers he had drawn it out and held it, by some inner prompting, between his dim eyes and the distant beacon, to find himself, an instant later, lying across his bed with two policemen in the room and the tread of his landlady's feet ascending the stairs. Even then, with no formulated ideas of the value of his discovery, instinct had warned him to slip the lens again into his pocket, and to their excited queries about where he had been and the manner of his return he had reiterated foolishly that he had been asleep. They had given him water—that of the strange ocean had been too brackish to drink—and bread, which he had devoured wolfishly, but to all their questions he had answered, 'I don't know. I was asleep,' until they finally left him, evidently much mystified, and whispering together.

It was during the ensuing night that, unable to sleep for thinking about the model fortress, he began to realise the almost unlimited possibilities it contained. In whatever uncharted spot the original was situated, he felt sure that its whereabouts remained undiscovered by man, and it followed logically that he would have unquestioned dominion there. True, there were no inhabitants upon whom to exercise it—but suppose he could find a way of transporting other people to the place? He had assured himself that the whole thing was not feverish delirium by making several more brief visits to the Keep, always being careful to maintain a tight hold on the lens when the period of black-out arrived. Reference to the alarm clock by his bed showed him that, whatever might be the distance from the model to the real fortress, the transit occupied no measurable time at all; and this fact alone, should he choose to defy mankind, would provide a perfect alibi, since no jury would admit that he could travel hundreds—maybe thousands—of miles in a fraction of a second. Any breach of law or convention would have to be carried out at the *real* place at a time when he was known to be at home, and this arrangement would safeguard him against its very discovery. He reverted to the problem of getting his victims—veritable slaves they would be— to the island of his sovereignty, and concluded that the lens was large enough for two people to look through it at once, if it were held at the right distance.

Peter awoke from a half-dream and smiled at the model. To this day he had never come an inch nearer to solving the location of Lost Keep itself, but the miniature had served him well, and he loved those early memories. How scornfully disbelieving his foreman had been when he had hinted at the acquisition of something with magical properties! It had required a lot of restraint and tact to persuade him round to the lodging-house for a demonstration after he had brusquely sacked Peter for failing to be at work on that memorable Monday, but Peter had feigned cheerful indifference, supporting his attitude with talk of a quite mythical better job waiting for him, and the mention of a bottle of whiskey, bought out of his slender savings, had clinched the matter. After a few drinks Peter had brought out the miniature and, inviting the foreman to sit beside him and concentrate upon it, had focused it with the lens. The usual enlargement of the image and the subsequent black-out had duly occurred, but this time, on coming to his senses in the great courtyard, he had seen beside him another figure—a figure with dropped jaw and blank eyes staring up at the colossal pile overhanging them. He had thereupon directed the lens at the beacon and translated himself back to Tilbury—alone.

It was only fair to himself, Peter always reflected at this point, to remember that he had been in ignorance of the man's alcoholic heart. He had intended to punish him by leaving him marooned for a day, and it was with no little horror—for his autocratic power was still new—that he found him lying dead at the gateway on the following morning. Assurance of immunity, however, had gone far to overcome any remorse he had felt, and the six pounds odd which he had found in the man's pockets had consoled him in his unemployment. Those six pounds had, in fact, been the foundation of his present fortune, for from that chance windfall the acquisition of other and larger sums had been a rational and easy step, and he had found that anything he carried on his person was translated with him on his journeys between Lost Keep and the everyday world. Other advantages, too, were afforded by his unique possession; there had been, for instance, women who had denied him.

On one thing Peter had always congratulated himself. He had never allowed any of his bond-slaves to escape from Lost Keep. Once, indeed, he had been tempted to bring back a girl, for whom he had felt an unusually lasting passion, into the warm world of sunlight and blue skies, but he had realised in time the danger of having his secret betrayed, and had left her to pine in the cold, grey twilight where none it seemed could survive more than a few months. He had taken her food and drink in plenty, for it had hurt him to visualise her in the agonies of starvation, but he had seen the lovely face grow wan, and the eyes lose a spark more of their lustre on each successive visit, and at the end he had stayed away for many days rather than face more of her pleadings for release.

Peter shook himself, and glanced at the clock. Knifton was nearly due. He had been sitting dreaming in his shirt-sleeves, for the evening was oppressively hot, and now he rose and donned a heavy silk dressing-gown that was hung over the back of his chair. It was a highly coloured affair, the fabric of which had been especially woven for him in a unique pattern of interlacing circles.

Lord Knifton was a man some fifty years of age, who possessed both personality and tact. Though he frankly disagreed with many of Peter's principles, and never hesitated to tell him so, when their joint affairs were involved, he had considerable respect for his business acumen, and liked him well enough socially. Thus it was that, on being shown into the library, he made no immediate attempt to introduce the subject of their recent dispute, but shook hands and accepted a cigar while chatting of generalities. He soon noticed the model fortress and remarked its brilliant workmanship.

'Yes,' Peter agreed, 'a marvellous example of miniature craft—but its wonders show up better when viewed through this glass. Just sit still and keep the model in focus. Don't look away even if it makes your head swim for a second. There's no danger to the eyes, and you'll find the effect amazing.' He leaned over the back of Lord Knifton's chair, and held the lens so that both could see the fortress through it.

'And now, Knifton,' he said stridently, 'I've got you just where I want you.'

His companion rubbed his eyes and looked about him in bewilderment. A moment ago he had been sitting in Hunt's luxuriously furnished library on a hot August night, looking at a miniature on the desk. Now, by some miracle, he found himself in a gigantic, stone-flagged court, high-walled, and fronted by a fortress of staggering dimensions, while, under a dead grey sky that cast no shadows, the windless air struck coldly through his thin evening suit. The stench of a charnel-house assailed his nostrils, and he saw with revulsion that the ground was strewn with human remains in all stages of decomposition from bare, bleached skeletons to gory carcasses of the freshly slain, and the less recently alive—hideously distended.

He cried out sharply, and recoiled several paces, slewing round with upraised arms as he collided with someone behind him.

'Only your host,' said the voice of Peter Hunt, with a chilly suavity from which all trace of friendliness had vanished, 'please make yourself *quite* at home. It *is* your home, now, you know—that is, until you realise that I'm bound to win in the end, and sign this concession you so smugly discountenanced yesterday.'

He produced an impressive looking document, stiff with seals, and opened it with a flourish, then, seeing that his guest remained tongue-tied, went on bitingly, 'Framing a spate of questions, I suppose? What's this place? How did I get here? And so forth. Well, you may save your breath. *Where* you are I know no better than you. What I do know is that I have been absolute monarch of it for many years. Peter Hunt of Park Lane, pillar of Society, political leader, supporter of the Constitution, deferring to the wishes of a dozen pettifogging public bodies—and enjoying the farce because I know that I can, at will, take any man to whose opinion I pretend to bow, and bring him here and *rule* him as *you* can rule a dog!' He laughed unpleasantly. 'You damned fool! Do you think it's for the money that I want your signature? I can get enough to pay the National Debt by bringing the rich to Lost Keep and stripping them of their wealth. There's one in there,' he muttered, as a despairing moan echoed from behind a barred grating in the stonework, 'he's trying to decide whether it's worth while to sign a cheque and write home to say how much he's enjoying his holiday—in Portugal! No, my esteemed and scrupulous partner, one grows weary of ruling over subjects a few at a time in this gloomy place. I want to come out into the open and rule a country—and when this concession goes through I can do it!'

At last Lord Knifton spoke, and in his tones were neither fear nor anger. Only an abiding sorrow.

'Peter Hunt,' he replied solemnly, 'by some diabolical means which I do not even wish to fathom you wield a power that no man is ready to possess. 1 can only say: God take that power from you before more evil is done!'

As he spoke a swift shadow blotted out half the sky, and Hunt threw back his head in amazement. In the whole course of his association with this weird retreat he had never known anything to break the canopy of twilight, and his hands fell nervelessly to his sides as there burst on his vision a mass of shining metal, so huge as almost to dwarf the Keep, miraculously suspended in space above it. For a few seconds its great spatulate point hovered over the turrets. Then, it darted down and rushed at them, its lower edge grinding and roaring along the paving stones.

'Uncle, you promised to show me your new microscope. May I see it now?' Pete demanded with a sidelong glance at his mother.

'But it's bedtime, dear,' said Lydia Hunt, 'and you can see Uncle Harry's reading. Run upstairs now like a good boy and you shall see it tomorrow.'

Pete drooped a pathetic lower lip. He was a sunny-natured child, though a trifle spoilt.

'Oh, but Uncle *did* promise. He *said* today, and I've been looking forward to it all school-time. I told the other chaps in our form about it, and they'll want to hear what I've seen with it tomorrow. Won't you show me something tonight *please*, Uncle Harry?'

Lydia's brother looked up from his evening paper with a whimsical smile. 'Well,' he laughed, 'I've promised to take it round to Dr. Pruden's tomorrow to check over some of his cultures, so perhaps the boy had better see it tonight. It won't take long. All right, Pete. The "mike's" in Daddy's library, and I believe he's got Lord Knifton there with him, but we'll see if they'll let us have it.'

Pete clutched one of his hands with the enthusiasm of the ten-year-old, and danced across the hall at his side. They came to the library door and knocked, but there was no reply. Pete pushed it open and looked in. 'Come on, Uncle Harry,' he cried, 'they must have gone out. Where's the microscope?'

His uncle crossed over to a cupboard, lifted out something large and shiny, and stood it on the desk. It was an expensive instrument, covered with exciting little brass knobs, and Pete's eyes gleamed when they saw it, 'Coo, what a beauty!' he exclaimed rapturously. 'Wish I had one!... Oh, and look, Uncle! Here's daddy's model fortress!

I've never seen it properly before. Can we look at *that* through the microscope?'

'No, of course not, you silly kid. They're for examining very tiny things like grains of dust, and you have to put them between the glass plates so as to light them from behind. If you just stood the end of the barrel against a lump of solid stuff you'd see nothing at all. Now then, here's a slide,' he went on, handing the boy two little oblongs of glass, 'just get a wee flake of dirt on the tip of that silver paper-knife and park it between these. Then I'll show you how the world looks to an influenza germ.'

Pete giggled, and scraped up a speck of dust from the courtyard of the model fortress, wiped the paperknife on the slide, and obediently passed it across. His uncle fitted it into a frame at the lower end of the barrel, bent down to the eye-piece and began manipulating the brass knobs. Pete watched him, fascinated, and chafed at the time it took to get the adjustment right. He was on the point of asking how soon he might be allowed to have a look when he heard his uncle give a low whistle.

'Pete,' he said, in a funny unsteady voice, and without lifting his head from the eye-piece, 'go and ask Mummy to come here, will you. And then hang on in the drawing-room till we call you, there's a good chap. I've got something I want her to see first, and after that you shall have the microscope to yourself till you go to bed.'

Though crestfallen at this further delay, Pete understood from the tone that it was not the time to argue, and presently Mrs. Hunt had taken his place by the desk. Her brother rose, and gave her a strange, searching glance.

'Take a look at that, old girl,' he suggested, indicating the microscope, 'and tell me if I'm dreaming.'

Lydia sat down in the chair. 'Why, Harry,' she exclaimed, 'they're miniature skeletons! But how on earth can they be modelled so perfectly on such a scale?'

Her brother shook his head. 'Pete certainly scraped that bit of dust off the miniature,' he answered. 'But they are not models! Take a grip on yourself, shift the slide from right to left. This is the button that operates it!'

Lydia obeyed the instruction and then broke out again in a tone of astonishment: 'But it's unbelievable! A pigmy race no bigger than bacilli, and shaped the exact pattern of humans? Why,' she added, 'there are even buckles and bits of cloth just like we wear. But they *must* be models!'

'Move the slide a bit further,' said Harry quietly, and then gripped her by the shoulders as she thrust her chair backwards from the desk with a cry of horror, cheeks blanched and eyes dilated.

'Harry! Harry!' she gasped, 'I can't bear it! It's Peter and Lord Knifton! That dressing-gown. There's not another like it in the world!... Oh, that horrible mess of blood... And the limbs were—were still *twitching!* What does it *mean?'*

Her brother poured some whiskey into a glass and held it to her lips. 'It means, I think, that there was truth in the legend of Lost Keep, and that Peter found the key. It would account for his mysterious disappearances—and other things!' he concluded grimly.

Lydia drained the tumbler and straightened up in the chair.

'You mean that the original castle really exists, and that, in some beastly fashion, its happenings are mirrored in the model?... Then tell me, Harry. How can we find the real place? There may still be life in them. We must send help. We *must!'*

Her brother sighed. 'There is no journey to make. How such a thing can be, God knows—but that thing is Lost Keep, and there they are locked—*multum in parvo*—Ugh! It makes me sick!'

Suddenly Lydia was galvanised into action. She began to turn out the drawers of the desk, scattering their contents on the carpet. 'The lens, Harry. The lens!' she cried hysterically. 'We can go ourselves and find out!'

Harry took her gently by the arm. 'No, dear,' he replied with finality, 'Peter has the lens.'

HYBRID

I HAVE KNOWN Billy Cole, or, to give him his proper title, Dr. X.W. Cole, M.D., M.R.C.S., since we were at school together. The 'X' stands for Xavier, a tradition in his family, but, of course, no one could be bothered with a mouthful like that.

He is, both in character and appearance, what one generally refers to as a 'hard case'. All doctors have to be, owing to their familiarity with pain and disease and the tragedy of their causes; but Billy is an exception even among his fraternity because most of his professional career has been spent in the capacity of a Ship's Surgeon in the Mercantile Marine.

Slight acquaintances get the impression that he is so calloused to human suffering and human vice as to be completely lacking in sympathy or sentiment, and indeed, his uncompromising, severely practical exterior supports the belief. In reality he is about the squar-est and whitest soul I know, and it is only his first-hand experience of life's seamy side among most of the world's races that has developed his iron self-control. I think he could hear or witness any conceivable horror literally without turning a hair.

On the occasion of his last shore leave prior to sailing for the Orient he followed his usual custom of spending a few days at my bachelor apartments in Town, and, as his arrival had been too late for me to organise a satisfactory 'night out', we were passing a quiet evening in my library over nuts and wine.

Since it will probably become self-evident later in the story, I may as well confess now to a strongly developed vein of morbid curiosity. Though I am pretty brawny in physique, I find something so uncanny in the actual spectacle of even a comparatively harmless lunatic as to give me feelings of absolute terror. At the same time maniacs and their more disgusting reactions hold me in a strange fascination.

I had been listening avidly to Billy's description of some of his most repulsive 'cases' when he concluded his recital with one about a dipsomaniac who ended his days chasing gigantic, violet wasps with a broom, and this yarn reminded me of some theories on the hallucinations accompanying 'D.T.s' which I had once heard in the course of an address by an eminent theosophical lecturer.

'Billy,' I asked him, without much expectation of tolerance from his pragmatic mind, 'do you think there may be anything in the occultist's notion that such monstrosities really *exist,* and are sometimes rendered visible through the medium of alcohol, drugs, and so forth?'

Much to my surprise, he accepted the suggestion without a trace of mockery, and answered with considerable gravity.

'You mean what they call breaking down the "web" that is supposed to divide the physical from the "astral". Well, when I was a student, I should have laughed like hell at any such idea. But— *experientia docet.* If you like, I'll tell you about another case that appeared to confirm that hypothesis. At all events, it had some aspects that were beyond ordinary pathological reasoning.'

'Fire away,' I invited eagerly, the morbid streak well to the fore. Billy settled himself deeper in his chesterfield and helped himself to a handful of nuts which he began cracking methodically, if absently.

'As far as I remember,' he began, 'we never had a schoolfellow named Chalmers—so I will call my "case" by that name. You see, the man in question *was* one of our contemporaries at St. Egbert's, and I've no doubt you'd remember him well enough, but it wouldn't be at all fair to him—or to his admirable wife—to give away their secret.

'Chalmers was, to all outward appearances, a perfectly normal, healthy boy, good at games to an average degree, passable in his form work, though not brilliant. I'm not a bit afraid of your recognising him from my description because he *was* so very average. He possessed one trait, though, of which I don't suppose anyone suspected him.

'Beneath his shell of seemingly thoughtless exuberance lay a deep strain of mysticism, all caused, so far as I could make out, by his having recurrent experiences of a singularly evil nightmare dating back to his very earliest recollections.

'I think I was his only confidant, though why he should have picked on me as recipient of his confidences I can't think. Fate, I imagine, and anyway it certainly helped me tremendously in understanding, his symptoms afterwards.

'Well, as Chalmers described it, he could not recall any time in his infancy when he was not haunted by an appalling fear—the worse because it was ill-defined—of some horrible entity constantly lurking near him. The usual childish dislike of darkness was, in his case, raised to the *nth* degree, so that he positively yelled with terror whenever he was left without light for a single instant. Up to the age of nearly nine he could not be induced to go to bed without a night-light, and a nurse or someone to share his room, but at about that period the new adventure of being sent to a day school and having a lot of fresh interests seems to have forced the thing into the back of his consciousness, where it remained for so long that he was finally able to forget it almost completely.

'He became quite a normal boy, swotted his subjects reasonably, played his cricket and football, and went to bed at night healthily tired, sleeping soundly without recourse to night-lights. When his mind did, very occasionally, turn to the presence that had haunted his cradle and cot, its nature had become so indistinct that, as he told me, he could not have described it even in the vaguest terms.

'Now, I'm sure you remember the phase we all went through at about fifteen when we fell easy prey to advertisers' announcements on the covers of penny "shockers", and were always wasting our pocket-money on dud water-pistols, electric tie-pins, et cetera. Some of us were most attracted by cheap-jack palmists and astrologers, and used to send in perfectly good half-crown postal orders together with time and place of birth in exchange for "an astounding character delineation and outline of your future". Chalmers belonged to this school of thought and must have spent pounds on being told to "beware of a dark woman", and all the usual bilge. He got fed up with it at last because, as he naively explained, no two forecasts corresponded.

'Now, personally, I'm inclined to think that, had he left fortune-telling alone for good, he might have grown up into an absolutely fit, sane, and unimaginative human animal, and saved himself the hell of a nasty experience later. But, as Fate would have it, a most superior sort of fair came to the town for a few days, and one of the side-shows was a booth tenanted by a self-styled lady psychometrist.'

'I remember,' I interrupted. 'Madame Caramel or Caramella or something.'

'Um. Name like that,' Billy agreed. 'Anyway, somebody persuaded Chalmers to give her a trial, and he duly paid his dollar and was taken into a dark room where the lady seated herself beside him on a divan and proceeded to hold his hand. He'd always had his fortune told by post before, and this method was a new one on him, with the result that he thought first of all she wanted him to make love to her. Being then about sixteen and unversed in the ways of the world, he was trying to decide how he ought to begin when the lady suddenly began talking at a rapid rate and squeezing his hand with a great access of muscular strength. Looking at her sharply, he saw that her eyes were shut and that her complexion had gone quite white, while beads of sweat stood out on the forehead. So greatly was he fascinated by his first experience of somebody in an apparently genuine trance that he missed quite a lot of her opening statements, but his ears were sharpened when she began telling him that his was a destiny of abysmal horror, and that his feet would walk forever in the glades of hell overshadowed by a sin-bred monster of his own begetting. He told me about the whole thing quite unexpectedly when we were out on a bird's-nesting ramble on a half-holiday, and, though he could not repeat the episode *verbatim*, the gist of it was that he had been addicted to the cult of Black Magic in a former life, and had begotten—or caused to be begotten—some dreadful hybrid, part human, part fowl, which looked to him for the continuity of its earthly existence, life by life, as he himself was reincarnate. That his "ego" had long since dropped the cult and was now concerned only with the processes of *natural* law did not free him from the responsibility for his "creature", and only by resuming his former malpractices at the cost of his own soul could he give this being its just chance of evolving through successive stages of bestiality until a wholly human vehicle could be attained.

'Well, that sort of thing at the time seemed to me the last word in tripe, apart from its degenerate aspect, and I told Chalmers so pretty bluntly. He retorted that he would certainly have thought the same, but for the fact that the psychometrist's affirmation had caused the resumption of his childish nightmares, and with greatly enhanced vividness.

'He was in a highly excitable state, and absolutely shouted down my arguments when he came to describe the thing that overshadowed him. He swore that it was the same apparition that had lurked long ago in his nursery, and described it as mainly human in shape, standing erect on legs, but entirely covered by silver-grey feathers except for the neck, which was naked and scrawny like that of a vulture. It loped rather than walked, and constantly tilted its feathered face to this or that side like a fowl when it is listening. Its eyes were jet-black and beady and filled with a febrile glee whenever they met his own. In spite of my youthful scepticism I found myself powerfully impressed by Chalmers' recital, and realised that his hallucination must, to him at any rate, be terribly existent. He became most convincing when he alluded to the creature's habit of hopping—or *fluttering*—on to his bed, and perching, with crossed legs, upon his chest. Several times, he maintained, he had dropped off to sleep through sheer weariness, awakening to find the monstrosity crouching above him, its restless, glinting orbs flickering rapidly from his head to his feet with an expression of conquering delight, as though it had, after long search, found its appointed resting-place. He went back to night-lights after that—not the old-fashioned wax wicks, but thirty-watt electric bulbs. The electric light switch in his bedroom remained depressed during the whole of his sleeping hours, and he craved for human companionship in those nocturnal stretches, though convention precluded the presence of a female nurse.

'You must understand that Chalmers was then going through a sort of private hell, and would have hated to take his people into his confidence for fear of ridicule. He could not, therefore, ask his brother to share his room, and must needs fight his own damnable destiny with his own resources.

'About twenty boys left St. E's at the end of that term—so you can amuse yourself guessing at Chalmers' identity. He was numbered among the twenty, and I didn't set eyes on him again for about two years, when I happened to bump across him in Oxford. No. He wasn't an "undergrad." His parents were both dead, and had left him enough money to treat Life as a kind of prolonged "Cook's Tour". That advantage didn't seem to have helped much. He had evidently undergone a tremendous change. In that brief period all his boyhood and good-nature had dropped away from him, and left a miserable, human hulk, unable—or unwilling—to discuss any ordinary human pleasantries, such as theatres, and concerned only with an abysmal introspectiveness.

'It was close to Carfax I met him, and, after listening to his sorrows as long as I thought judicious, I took him into the first licensed restaurant I could think of—it happened to be the "George"—and bought him a feed, complete with alcoholic extras. That didn't seem to do him much good, and, having ascertained that he was temporarily residing at the "Crown and Thistle" at Abingdon, I ran him home in my car. That was the last I saw of Chalmers for about twelve years, and by the time I next heard of him both the man and his delusion had pretty well faded from my memory.

'It was during one of my visits to the old people at their house near Worcester that our paths crossed again, and it happened in this way. The governor, as you know, still keeps his practice going, and we were discussing one of his invalids at a rather late hour one evening in his study.

'The housemaid presently announced a lady visitor whom she had shown into the consulting-room, and the Pater, who is very easy-going about surgery hours, went straight in to see her. He came back almost at once, however, and told me I was the doctor she wished to see.

'This surprised me a bit as, apart from giving the old man occasional advice with some difficult case, I had never been concerned in his practice and was, in fact, very rarely at liberty to go and stay with him.

'The girl who confronted me was tall and well formed, her untouched complexion testifying to a country upbringing. She introduced herself, without preamble, as Mrs. Cyril Chalmers, and said how thankful she was that I happened to be on shore leave. She looked intelligent and level-headed, though her face showed lines of worry, and I noticed—it is a doctor's job to notice such things—that she was about to become a mother. Chalmers and his obsession came back to me as soon as she mentioned the name, but I quite naturally supposed that it was about her pregnancy she wished to consult me. This supposition was strengthened when she asked how soon my leave expired, and I told her I still had three weeks to go.

'"In that case," she went on, "perhaps you wouldn't mind attending to my confinement, but it's really about Cy that I've come to see you. He tells me you know all about the thing which he believes overshadows him."

'I nodded, and she gave me a look of relief. "That helps," she continued, "because, when I tell you that the thing has mastered him and turned him into a raving lunatic, you'll understand how to approach his case, He's been completely uncontrolled for months now, and the only reason I've been able to keep him at home is because he hasn't actually attacked anyone—at least not murderously. I've had to get rid of all female servants, you understand, and our staff now consists of two ex-service men, one acting as male nurse and the other as cook-general. Of course, I could quite easily get him certified and put in a mental home, only it's sometimes difficult to get a patient out again, even when they are cured. Often I fear he is incurable, but you will be a better judge of that, and if there is any treatment available for such a case I'd like it done at home. Cy takes the same view, but doesn't want to be attended by anyone but yourself. He has great faith in you."

"'Oh,'" I interrupted, "he has lucid intervals, then?" But she shook her head vigorously. "No," came her flat denial. "He is *constantly* 'possessed'. He keeps hopping and sidling about like some horrible crow, and even in his sleep he looks only half human."

"'Then how was he able to direct you to me?" I naturally enquired, and received the astonishing reply, "*His body is mad, but his mind is sane.*"

"'What the devil do you mean?" I asked sharply, for this crazy statement sounded suspiciously like a leg-pull.

'She answered in a perfectly calm voice, and I began to admire her level-headedness, though I was badly puzzled.

"'You'll understand when you see him, doctor. The fact is, he doesn't realize what has happened. All the time he is strutting and flapping about the place he can talk and answer questions in his own perfectly normal voice, but he doesn't seem to know that *his* vocal cords are uttering the words. He speaks as though he were in some other part of the room watching the antics of his own body. It is quite evident after a few moments' conversation that he has some extraordinary sense of standing outside himself and looking on. He thinks his body is the creation that haunts him!"

'I kept silent a few minutes while I tried to take this in. It was a new kind of delusion in my experience.

"'Well,'" I suggested at length, "you'd better tell me how the whole business started." And it was in giving the account of this that her admirable poise *did*, for a short time, desert her. I found ample excuse, though, when I'd heard the facts. The ordeal that poor girl had gone through would have driven ninety per cent. of women straight off their heads.

'Apparently she and Chalmers had met at a dance about two years before and fallen in love, more or less at first sight. As he had plenty of money there was no reason for a long engagement, though Chalmers was sensible enough to tell his fiancée about his secret fear and the words of the fortune-teller before the wedding. He assured her there was no hereditary insanity in his family, and that his delusion—if delusion it was—could hurt nobody but himself, adducing the fact that no other person had ever been able to see his spectre even though it presented itself to his own perceptions in crowded places. The girl was pleased at this display of his confidence, which made her all the more eager to marry him as she believed her companionship would be a help when he thought the apparition was nearby. The ceremony was therefore hastened on, and for several months it *did* seem that the acquisition of a wife had improved Chalmers' spirits. He began to go about much more than he had done for years, taking his wife on a constant round of theatres, dances, and bridge-parties. He even voluntarily alluded to his obsession, and she realised that his choice of such a gay life was prompted by his desire for distraction from it.

'The only inconvenience she suffered was having to get used to sleeping with a light on.

'Well, they kept up a protracted honeymoon for a considerable time, travelling a lot, and staying at all the most expensive hotels. The girl—a country parson's daughter—had never lived so lavishly before, and she enjoyed every bit of it.

'At last, however, she suggested that they ought to take a house somewhere and settle down for a bit, if only to return the hospitality they had been receiving from Chalmers' wealthy acquaintances, and the place they picked was an old Victorian mansion in a Sussex village not too far from Town.

'The furnishers and decorators had it ready for them in a few weeks, and they celebrated their entrance into County life by throwing a big house-party to which a number of Bright Young People were invited. Everything seems to have gone with a swing from start to finish, the Bright Young People inventing their own amusements from day to day and thus saving host and hostess a lot of organising.

'Mrs. Chalmers, however, noticed from the outset that her husband's recent gaiety was on the decline. He entered into various round games and skylarks when he was literally cornered by his guests, but, as often as opportunity offered, he would slip out unobserved and wander off into the country for hours on end, frequently not returning till the small hours of the morning. He began to suffer badly from insomnia, but turned down all suggestions that he should try sleeping draughts. Mrs. Chalmers was constantly waking up in the night to find him sitting in a chair reading, and her woman's instinct finally brought her to the realization that he was *frightened to sleep.*

'One morning when he came home after three and found her lying awake she took him to task about it. He was more fidgety and *distrait* than ever, and his eyes had a wild expression like those of something hunted.

'"Really, my dearest," she began, "you were sweet to tell me all about your trouble when we were engaged. What have I done to lose your confidence now? I could see for myself that, whatever your delusion, you weren't mad, and that was why I never hesitated to marry you. But, if you don't get a doctor to give you a sleeping mixture you'll go mad. What is there about this place that's upsetting you? You were all right until we came here."

'Chalmers, it seems, suddenly broke down, burst into tears, and went off into a long disjointed account of having found the monster's home.

37

'"I felt certain I recognized this place when I first saw it," he concluded, "and I hadn't been in it many hours before I began to get flashes of having lived here before—not in this life, but centuries ago. I remembered vaguely on the second evening of our residence some *outré* event having taken place in these very grounds, though the house wasn't there then. I think it happened in some kind of marquee bearing heraldic signs. There was much consternation among a group of priests, and something was put to death and buried in a field about a mile away. I recall being forced to march in the procession to the burial ground, and after that—it's all hopelessly confused—but I—I *think I was burnt at the stake.*"

'He shivered and threw himself face down across the bed while his anxious wife soothingly stroked his hair.

'"I found the field that same night," he continued brokenly, "and the thing rose up out of the ground to meet me. It's got a hypnotic hold on me and forces me to go night after night to commune with it. As soon as it appears I fall into a kind of stupor and can see nothing clearly, though I have a dreadful remembrance after of having stood for hours on end in a rustling, *feathery* embrace. I don't know what the thing does to me, but I am falling more and more into its spell, and I have no volition to resist."

'He sobbed again convulsively, and then muttered in scarcely audible tones: "In a way I'm even beginning to *like* it! At first I felt that it was angry with me for not giving it a beastly, *hybrid* vehicle for the accomplishment of its desires. Now it seems content with our loathsome communions."

'You can well picture poor Mrs. Chalmers' state of mind when she heard this confession. As she saw it, her husband was now definitely suffering from a serious dementia, but she realized how impossible it would be to get his consent to medical advice, and how futile it was to argue with him.

'She uttered no word of criticism, but quietly and firmly made up her mind to follow him to his next assignation and see for herself what he did. Their house-party was now almost broken up, and she had no great difficulty in slipping out of a side-door that evening, dressed in a dark, inconspicuous costume, and following Chalmers along a thickly hedged lane to a five-barred gate over which he proceeded to climb. He had marched all the way like a sleep-walker without once turning his head, and she now contrived to follow him into the field, where she concealed herself in the moon-shadow of a broad and leafy elm. She saw Chalmers march mechanically on and halt in the middle of the meadow, where he stood with outstretched arms as though awaiting the embrace of some invisible being. For some ten minutes he remained thus unmoving. Then all at once he seemed to divine her presence, though how he could have seen her in the shadow at such a distance, and with his back towards her, she could not fathom. She only knew that he had turned about and was dashing with unbelievable speed straight for her hiding-place. She stood rooted there, utterly paralyzed with terror, for, instead of the square-shouldered, nimble sprint she had so often admired on the tennis courts, he was coming in a series of fluttering, sidelong hops instinct with the vigorous intensity of a ravening vulture. Within what seemed a second of time he was upon her and, seizing her in a grip of abnormal strength, had thrown her to the ground. So, with one sinewy hand on her throat, he held her pinned, while the other, fingers crooked like talons, ripped and tore at her clothing. Her whirling senses shrieked to her that this was not her husband suddenly demented, but an entirely alien presence into which he had been transformed. Her struggles and attempts to cry out were rendered futile in that merciless grip, and she could only lie supine with eyes fast shut to keep out the terror of the metamorphosed face, while in her nostrils clung a farmyard reek, and weird croakings and twitterings assailed her ears. Then her senses left her completely.

'When she came to she was still lying in a bed of long, dewy grass in the shadow of the elm, her clothes torn to shreds and her body bruised from head to foot. Of Chalmers there was no sign. Fortunately a long silk opera cloak she had been wearing had fallen from her at the first onslaught and escaped damage. She was able to conceal the remnants of her costume beneath it, and to reach the house without exciting comment.

'Now, I think she proved herself a very courageous gentlewoman when she made her way to their bedroom by the back-stairs without seeking the aid of guests or servants. On trying the door she found it locked, but, at the rattle of the handle, her husband's voice—now absolutely normal—came from within.

'"You can't come in, dear," he said earnestly, "the Thing has come back with me, and it won't leave."

'"Nonsense," she replied with firmness, "I must come. Don't you know you've hardly left a rag of clothes on me?"

'"I've *what*," he shouted incredulously, "what d'you mean? I haven't even seen you since tea!" The apparent sanity of his tone helped her courage. Chalmers must have been quite unconscious of his actions in the field.

'"I must come in," she repeated, "never mind what you've got in there with you. I must help you fight it."

'She heard the lock click and a scamper of footsteps crossing the floor. She pushed the door open, slammed it behind her, and stood leaning back against it, her frightened gaze resting on the astounding spectacle before her.

'Attired in purple pyjamas, and holding in his mouth a wriggling garden worm, Chalmers was hanging by both hands and one bare foot from the bedrail in the attitude of a parrot that clings inverted to the top of its cage.

'"You see," he remarked courteously, the worm dropping to the floor as his lips opened, "the beastly thing's got in here now and pinched a suit of my pyjamas."

'He dropped to the floor, twisting in agile fashion to alight upon his feet, and hopped upon the window-sill, where he perched with his head askew, and went on conversationally, "Now that you've seen it with your own eyes I need evade the subject no longer. Here it is— even contriving to look something like me—and here it undoubtedly means to stay unless we can think of some way to get rid of it. Two heads better than one, eh, dear?"

'He stopped for a moment, scratched the back of his ear with one big toe, and continued: "I wouldn't mind so much if the brute would keep still sometimes, but it won't. It seems imbued with an eternal energy, and keeps hopping about as you can see." As he spoke he sprang from the sill to the top of a big walnut wardrobe and perched there.

'Mrs. Chalmers' face became more composed as an idea presented itself. "Its movements are so quick," she remarked, "that they distract my attention from you. Would you mind telling me where you were standing, for instance, when it made the last move?"

'Chalmers' voice sounded sulky and irritable as he answered her.

'"You little idiot! I wasn't standing. I've been sitting here on the bed ever since you came in." But the voice came from the grotesque figure on the wardrobe.

'Well, that is as much as I need tell you about the origin of Chalmers' dementia,' said Billy, mechanically shelling another nut.

'Chalmers refused to occupy the same bedroom with his wife because, as he explained, he could not get rid of his uncanny visitant, and it was not proper that she should robe and disrobe in its presence—an opinion for which the poor lady was devoutly thankful.

'We put her up for the night, and the next day I travelled with her to her Sussex home to interview the patient. He—or rather his body—was in a recalcitrant state when I was shown in. The nurse, a big brawny fellow, told me that it had been the devil's own job to prevent his escaping that morning when he heard that his wife was still away. Even primed with Mrs. Chalmers' account of her husband's delusion, I will confess that it gave me an uncanny feeling to see the fellow strutting and pirouetting obscenely while his voice said in perfectly natural accents: "Glad you could come, Cole, but take no notice of that idiot."

"'I wasn't trying to escape. It was the blasted hybrid, and, if they let it, there'll be hell popping. Not a woman in the village will be safe from what I can guess of its instincts." I noticed that Chalmers' face was heavily coated with cream and talcum powder so that he looked unpleasantly like a sex pervert.

"'Why do you—?" I began, and then hastily remembered his delusion. "Why does your hybrid put that stuff on its face?" He hopped several times from floor to bed and back again before replying.

"'It imitates me," he said, "in every little thing I do. It uses my safety razor—only it has to remove not hair, but *feathers*. I suppose it puts the cream and talcum on to hide the quills."

'I shivered a bit, and soon made a pretext to leave him.

"'Mrs. Chalmers," I told his wife, as soon as we were out of earshot, *there* is no need to get your husband certified, but I absolutely insist upon his leaving this house until your confinement is over.

Now I've a friend—a Dr. Gunter—who keeps a private nursing home not many miles from here. We shall have to drug Cyril and take him there in a closed car, Gunter will look after him until you're on your feet again, and then you can bring him back here—if you still wish to.'

'To my relief, she fell in with the proposal, and that afternoon the plan was put into effect. For once Chalmers seemed to realise that he was in some way identified with his "hybrid", for he shouted at me to get to hell out of it for a treacherous hound, while I was adjusting the chloroform pad.

'I stayed on at the house to keep an eye on the wife until her time came, and then 'phoned Gunter, asking him to come over as assistant. You see, I had found out that Mrs. Chalmers' pregnancy dated from the night of his metamorphosis, and had decided to administer an anaesthetic.

'It would be as well, I thought, if she *saw* nothing.

'Well, the event finally took place, and my watch told me the hour was two a.m. We removed the—er—offspring to an adjoining room, where it lived only for a few hours. Confidentially, we made no very serious effort to save its life, and it was just as we had finally ascertained that the pulse had really stopped that a 'phone call came in from Gunter's Matron to say that Chalmers had suddenly recovered his sanity. One of his first acts had been to wipe the powder from his face with a handkerchief, and he had then called an attendant, to whom he expressed his satisfaction that the "hybrid" had all at once dissolved into thin air, leaving him with a greater sense of freedom and well being than he had known for months.

'As it happened, Gunter was then washing his hands, and it was I who took the call. Something prompted me to enquire the hour at which Chalmers had been restored, and the Matron replied that, to the best of her knowledge, it was about two a.m.

'Now then, you can call me imaginative if you like, old man, but *I believe* that there *was* something from "the other side" attached to Chalmers, and that it did actually steal his body for a period of time. When the offspring was born its needed vehicle was to hand, and into it the non-human strain passed from Chalmers through the medium of his wife. Evidently it could not get back when the infant body died, and I think that, with Chalmers' debt of suffering paid in full, Providence may have mercifully allowed the hybrid soul to die too. I shall never forget the venom with which its new-born eyes looked at me while I withheld the nourishment it needed.'

Billy stopped and took a sip of port, but my morbid streak was not yet satisfied. 'But what was the offspring *like?*' I demanded.

Billy shot me an amused glance. 'Thank God it was passably human in *shape,*' he responded, 'but we had to *pluck* it before the undertakers came.'

THE TOWER OF MOAB

MY INTRODUCTION to The Tower of Moab came about in the course of travelling salesmanship. It is not, I take it, strange that I had never previously heard of the place, since the local residents are hardly aware of its existence, save as a familiar land-mark, and, incidentally, a fare-stage for buses. I dare say it is not sufficiently historical to be widely known, whilst yet past its prime as the 'Nine days' wonder' it must once have been. All the same, in these times of cheap public transport thousands of people from all parts must constantly be seeing it: and, to my mind, it would be odd if they failed to mention it in their home towns as something of a national curiosity. I may of course be prejudiced by its special signifi-cance to myself, and yet I want to make it very plain that when I first set eyes on it I saw it only as a rather unexpected ruin remarkably unblemished by Time. I use the word 'unexpected', because the place is situated quite near the centre of one of our minor industrial towns close to the crossing of two main roads where every yard of land must be worth a good deal for shops, flats, and so forth. Indeed, the base of the Tower is entirely surrounded by such buildings, which may account in part for the scant heed paid to it, since, like the cathedrals of Canterbury, Peterborough and many other cities, it is quite visible from the adjoining thoroughfares, and its ragged summit, viewed from a greater distance across the sea of roofs, tends to lose interest with absence of detail.

I was 'travelling' in the neighbourhood, as I have already stated, one of the numerous things I had tried since the War with fairly consistent non-success.

My parents had been killed in an air-raid, and the paternal capital, once of comforting dimensions, was brightening the life of Russia—hence a series of diverse and badly-paid jobs, the one of the moment happening to be salesmanship. Like the rest, it appeared almost to have run its course, and, with about one order to my credit for a three weeks' tour, I was anticipating the firm's valediction at any moment. There was one more call to be made to complete my list for the district, and through it "The Tower of Moab" was first mentioned to me. I was directed to take a bus and dismount there for the shop I wanted. Feeling curious about the odd title of the place, I asked the conductor what it was, and was informed that some obscure, religious sect had started to build it, less than a century ago, with the idea of continuing its elevation until, like Babel, it should reach heaven. By all accounts funds had become exhausted and the monument was discontinued after attaining to a height of some two hundred feet. The cult had also died out, ostensibly for the same reason, but, owing to the phenomenal strength and massiveness of their handiwork, the cost of clearing the site for new buildings would not be justified. More than this my informant could not tell me, and having alighted there I caught my first glimpse of the Tower through a narrow alley between two blocks of houses—just the top part with its uneven sky-line, dentured as the workmen had left it, and with not even the dignity of age to tone down its crude yellow tint.

I had little difficulty in finding the required address, and encountered the usual reception. The proprietor was too busy to see me. Now, in my probationary week at the show-rooms I had been schooled in various methods of dealing with this form of passive resistance, and by the exercise of 'Blandishments 1 to 5 on the Syllabus' I finally succeeded in entering the Presence, who, clearly annoyed by the failure of his assistant to get rid of me, wasted some ten minutes of his valuable time in telling me that he was perfectly satisfied with existing supplies and was damned if he would open any fresh accounts—all with the most deliberate offensiveness. And this after I had toiled from place to place in grilling heat, lugging a heavy case of samples! Undoubtedly someone had upset the man earlier in the day, and I only mention him to illustrate how the reaction of one tempera-ment to another may in turn affect a third, and how he was thus the unwitting link joining my former purely material life to that menacing shadow realm in which I now walk.

Thoroughly disgusted with his disheartening treatment, sick of genuine endeavour, and weary to the depths of my soul at the ever-lasting uncharitableness of mankind, I responded to an inherited trait which never obtruded itself on me in moments of success.

I walked straight from that shop into the nearest public house, threw my bag on a settee in the saloon bar and began to drink.

The room into which I had rather unnoticingly wandered was admirably suited to the mood that possessed me. In the first place it was empty, and, in the second, its one tall window faced the counter, whilst in the corner between it and the fireplace was one of those rail backed, leather-covered settees, long enough to accommodate about three people. By occupying one end of this and using the other as a leg-rest I could enjoy the combined privileges of having the light at my back, standing my glass on the window-sill, commanding a good view of the barmaid for purposes of effortless replenishment, and deterring any chance newcomer from sitting sufficiently near me to start a conversation. Though by no means a misanthrope, I was never one of those gregarious souls who expand in direct ratio with the number of their immediate neighbours.

That day in particular, discouraged by years of drudgery, and furiously angry with the object of my last visit, I wanted above all

47

things to be left alone, and it was with relief that I saw the barmaid surreptitiously produce some paper-backed 'thriller' from under the counter, as soon as she had served me my drink. I had chosen to sit with my face in the shadow because I realised that I was in all likelihood scowling like a stage villain, and it would have upset me inordinately had I thought the girl would observe it and imagine I was being theatrical. Neither did I wish her to see some unconscious mannerism displayed, leading to the suspicion that I was a common toper. I was sensitive on the point, for normally I had the craving well in hand until some rebuff brought out a spirit of savage recklessness from below the surface.

That Saturday morning in July I sat in the grimy little bar, gradually stimulating myself to the pitch when I could put away the petty irritations of my job, my lack of capital, and general burden of ill-luck, and rise into the Nirvana of concentrated, objective thought. Eight or nine double Scotches served to bring this about, save for a dull resentment that fate should compel me to take my pleasures in so squalid a place, instead of in the dignity and comfort of some state-ly country home. I glanced furtively at my reflection in the overman-tel mirror to make sure that my features were suitably composed and showed no trace of what I had consumed before strolling to the counter to study a time-table. As I did so, I caught a reflection on the opposite pavement, and above, through the same alley I had previously noticed, an angle of The Tower of Moab, shining vivid yellow in a watery gleam of sunlight.

What an extraordinary conception it was, to be sure, for a group of almost present-day people to indulge. I thought over the bus con-ductor's summary and half decided to broach the subject to Hebe in the hope of gleaning further data, but decided that it would probably elicit more small-talk than I wanted. Anyway, I already possessed the main facts, which were enough food for speculation. I tried to recall the story of Babel from the Old Testament, but found that, after the fashion of post-war Europe, I had so long neglected church-going and religious discourse that most of it had faded from my memory in common with Jonah, David and Goliath, and the rest of the Sunday School favourites. Assuming, though, that Babel was historical fact and not a myth, I could fancy the relatively ignorant people of that time attempting to reach the sky under the impression that it was solid, but how anyone could entertain such a notion after balloonists had disproved it, was beyond my comprehension. I myself had been a scout pilot in the Flying Corps, and in the habit of flying at altitudes of more than twenty thousand feet, and the whimsical idea struck me that plans for a tower at least fifty thousand feet in height would be needed to persuade an airman that there was still territory to explore. Though no architect, I realised the hopelessness of designing a base that would stand the weight, and further supposed that the Earth's rotation would bend such an edifice like a whisker. No doubt, though, there had been and still were plenty of fools who would give money for a project of this kind through their ignorance of mechanical laws, especially in the name of a religious belief. One could, in fact, picture the founder of the creed, Elder, or whatever he called himself (almost certainly in the building and contracting line), collecting subscriptions with his tongue in his cheek and telling his disciples that in a matter of forty years they could enter Paradise without the painful necessity of dying.

I decided to go out and have a closer look at the means.

When I finally stood at the base of the Tower and gazed up at it, I was chiefly struck by the incongruity of its surroundings. It was the sort of erection one would have looked for on some windswept and desolate hill where its devotees could get the atmosphere of walking with God in the high places; and yet here, once approached, it was even more arresting in its ability to preserve a very real dignity, despite its prosaic background. Almost, indeed, one ceased to hear the traffic or to see anything beyond the mass of this gigantic hollow pillar. For that was its simple form—four walls with a base perhaps fifty yards square and forming a plain, vertical shaft. It had no interior decoration, neither was there evidence of galleries nor even a stairway. I wondered how the builders had raised the large blocks of masonry, and supposed they had hauled them up with ropes and pulleys.

If the inside of the shaft was uninteresting, the exterior most certainly made up for it; and passing out through one of the small archways in the base of the walls I crossed to one side of the island of wasteland in which it stood, and made a slow circuit of it.

Groups of dirty children were playing here and there among piles of old tins and rubble, and I saw a few slatternly women looking down at me from the windows of tenements which backed on to the shops and better-class houses of the street; but these hardly penetrated my consciousness, so absorbed was I in the huge scale designs which began nearly a hundred feet above my head. The ugly yellow colour that had first caught my eye was, I found, the pigment of some kind of cement, presumably very hard, since it showed little sign of cracking after seventy or eighty years of weather, and with this the whole was covered, forming a medium of tiers of elaborate moulding and scroll-work at intervals of ten feet. The upper portion of each wall blossomed into a panel at least fifty feet high, representing some scene out of Biblical history or The Revelations and executed in the same cement modelling. One looked like the Archangel Gabriel sounding the Last Trump with an immense horn, out of which poured a volume of Hebrew script, whilst round the corner on the next face, was a tumultuous scene so crowded with figures as to defy interpretation, but probably depicting the Day of Resurrection. What the others were I forget, but at all events each had the quality of impressing, partly by reason of its height from the ground, its gargantuan execution, and its literal reading of what I had always vaguely regarded as allegorical. One gets something of this feeling from the prints in an old Family Bible in which the air is full of the most substantial-looking winged angels, and there is a pit full of demons in the foreground. I think that young children, being shown such things, go about thereafter expecting to meet them.

I had been gazing up at the figures and ruminating along such lines for longer than I realised when the Tower of Moab worked its first spell on me. The sun was now shining with considerable heat and brilliance after a mostly overcast and showery morning, and if it was this, coupled with the amount of whisky I had consumed, or was just the effect of staring too long against the bright sky, I did not know; but I experienced one of those alarming optical phenomena which one associates with liver disorders, and found a sort of blackness descending on all objects to left and right, bringing an instant feeling of faintness and causing my eyes to water violently. It only lasted a moment, during which I steadied myself on my stick with the natural instinct not to attract attention by collapsing in public. But in that instant came a swiftly passing and awful sense of despair, and the words rushed into my head, 'My God. It *does* reach to Heaven!'

Exactly why that thought arose I cannot possibly say, for at that time I am positive my *eyes* had registered nothing supernatural. Most probably it was the inner working of intuition warning me of something monstrous and intimately bound up with my life.

Having now missed two trains and feeling that one place was as

51

good as another for a lonely week-end, I decided to remain where I was until the Monday morning and then catch an early train to get me to the office by nine o'clock. This move would save me the trouble of posting the firm that night, as I should be able to forestall the mail and make my report personally.

I may as well also admit to a desire to complete what I had begun in the public-house without the staling effect of an interruption, for it has always been my way after starting an orgy to finish the job properly. The craving, in fact, which is non-existent for the first three or four drinks, appears strongly after half a dozen.

My problem was to secure a room at a place where I could get as much as I wanted to drink without having to fetch it, and without the necessity of smuggling it to bed and pleading sickness. The notion of lying in bed to take whisky robs the beverage of its whole charm, nor do I care about having it in a bedroom at all, even sitting up and fully dressed. A licensed hotel, therefore, appeared the best solution, and, at that, one of the largest places, where an ample staff would supply me legally at any hour without raising its eyebrows. But, as it transpired, I was saved the bother of a search, for, on returning to my first port of call in time to 'wedge a couple' before the closing hour, the landlord said he could give me a top room for as long as I liked, with access to his second floor private sitting-room which, he told me, he never used. Of course, the place was not residential, but this suited me all the better, as I ran no risk of bumping into acquaintances, whilst the saving of money was a consideration, the landlord being a sportsman and agreeing to the moderate figure of three shillings for the night. Being, moreover, a publican, he would not care what I drank provided that I did not become a nuisance.

Having heard a few tap-room customers depart and seen all the street doors locked, I followed him up to the sitting-room, which proved to be quite a comfortable place, well carpeted and with some good armchairs, where I proceeded to establish myself in the right way by ordering a bottle of whisky and two glasses. My normal manner of reserve being now dissipated by my previous potations, I was able to keep him thoroughly amused for quite an hour, and I feel sure he took it in the right spirit, when, at the end of that period, I tactfully explained that I did a lot of writing in my spare time and would like to be left pretty much alone for the rest of that day and Sunday. This would allow me full rein for my greatest relaxation, slowly stimulating my thoughts to farther and farther flights till I felt like a colossus of wisdom dominating the Globe, but with no fear of those irritating interruptions occasioned, for instance, by well-meaning people saying it is cold for the time of year just when I am nearing a conclusion on the possibilities of Mormonism as a workable social basis.

As my new friend went out, I asked him with studied casualness to send me up another bottle, adding that I was accustomed to it, and that it clarified my mind wonderfully for my work. I think he was sincere in replying that he took his hat off to a gentleman who could put it away like me, and reflected that the barmaid must have mentioned my morning session, since I had only had half a bottle in his company. This, I admit, tickled my vanity, for I consider fighting the stupefying effect of alcohol to be about the finest test of will-power.

Hitherto, I had had no ill results, my constitution throwing off a carouse reliably and well. Hence, it annoyed me to find on crossing the room that, on this occasion, there was evidently something wrong with my liver.

The Tower of Moab loomed in full view above the opposite house by reason of my two-storey climb, and, as I glanced across and took in a general impression of its yellow mass against an indefinite blue background streaked with smoke, once more the pall of blackness crept in from the tail of my eyes, leaving nothing else in the picture. Then a great flash of brilliant white light seemed to spread fanwise from the bridge of my nose, and through it and among it, to my distorted vision, the Tower seemed to grow beyond all dimensions of human conception, until it reared its ragged neck illimitably into the sky's vault. Next, numberless bright stars fell slowly, curtain like, between me and it, and the moment after, I was back in a chair, seeing the room as usual and controlling, for the benefit of the girl who appeared with my next bottle, a desire to breathe gustily through the mouth. I fancied, however, that she looked at me queerly as she withdrew, as though awaiting something, and my next actions would, I think, have proved interesting to any observer. They fascinated one half of my own mind, which was just then studying my body's movements with an introspective, but amazingly lucid detachment.

I waited until the servant's footfalls had receded into the distance, and then walked quietly up to my bedroom, where I carefully washed my face and hands in cold water before returning to the sitting-room and uncorking the fresh bottle of whisky. This done, I poured out a tumbler full of the neat spirit, placed it carefully on the table, and moved across to a hanging mirror in which I studied myself, and more particularly my eyes, for several minutes. The mirror reflected my face clearly without blurring, and showed that the eyes were steady and the pupils neither unduly dilated nor contracted. Next, I picked up a newspaper and methodically read a paragraph of small type while holding it at arm's length. Satisfied with the result of these tests, I recrossed to the window, where I must have remained staring upwards for at least ten minutes, at the end of which I again seated myself, picked up my glass of whisky and settled down to face the greatest problem of my life.

And it was a problem indeed, for, whilst after my strange optical illusion all other objects within the room and outside had resumed their usual aspect, The Tower of Moab had not! It remained, as in that revealing moment it had grown, a colossal fantastic thing, rising infinitely high into the blue upper air from its foundations among the commonplace brick buildings and roofs of slate. And past it, to and fro along the drab pavements, went the inevitable crowd of shoppers and idlers—seeing nothing new. And to and fro likewise, in the midway of the road, went trams, buses, taxis and private cars, their occupants intent upon their immediate purposes, moving as ever importantly about their business, unaware of the great unearthly column that now towered above them like the finger of God uplifted in warning.

I forget whether it was that evening or in the small hours of the Sunday morning that I reached my decision to stay on and learn more of this awful and stupendous thing of which I had been granted vision. Certainly it was on the Sunday afternoon that I took pen and paper and wrote to my employers, furnishing an account of my calls for the week and pointing out that I had realised my incompetence for the task which they had set me, and was therewith tendering my resignation in fairness to themselves. As a sop to my conscience, and to carry out the gesture which it seemed essential to their recognition of my integrity, I enclosed a cheque to the value of two weeks' wages with an apology for leaving them without due notice. This they returned, as I supposed, in that spirit of pique which is even more peculiar to the dignity of a limited liability company than to that of an individual. To my landlord I explained that my departure would be indefinitely postponed owing to the praiseworthy privacy of his rooms which permitted me to concentrate on my literary work better than I had been able to do elsewhere. I fancy he was flattered, and, in any case, he was not likely to wish me to go, since I had paid a week in advance and was at pains to see that no disturbance took place even when, at intervals, alcohol got the better of me, as it was bound to do under such conditions of mental strain.

As day succeeded day, I became more adapted to the extraordinary, but publicly unknown fact of the Tower's existence as a finished work. In the first week I secured various textbooks published by the Theosophical Society and kindred bodies, and refreshed my memory upon a fund of subjects once half studied in the wayward fashion of youthful curiosity. One paragraph in particular I unearthed from a tome entitled *Nature Spirits and Thoughtforms* and underlined. It ran as follows—

'It must never be forgotten that the most transitory, trivial thought born of a human mind is as real and lasting a thing as a house built of stones and mortar. It is not just an impalpable vision illuminated for so long as the mind retains it, but a positive creation that lives on after the creator has consciously forgotten it, for a period proportionate to its own strength. Hence it has been asserted by numerous clairvoyants that the perpetual, concerted faith of devotees in the idolatrous gods of ancient Egypt actually created such beings and endowed them with minds far out-reaching those of their creators, and vital force enabling them to exist through the centuries even down to the present day!'

Applying this principle, a plausible one enough, I concluded that for some reason I had been suddenly invested with clairvoyant perception and had become aware of The Tower of Moab as conceived in the minds of its founders and completed on the astral plane after its physical growth had stopped.

During the second week I purchased a pair of field-glasses, and spent hours at the sitting-room window scrutinising the higher faces of the Tower and the fresh mural panels gradually unfolding above me. I realised the futility of taking anyone into my confidence, and, in order to carry out my design without attracting unwelcome attention from passers-by, I used to lower the Venetian blind during the sunny hours on the pretext of keeping out the heat and conduct my investigations between the slats. At night, however, after the household was in bed, I would come down from my back room and sit with the blind up, gazing at the vast bulk of the Tower, which then stood black and menacing, like some giant chimney, its top lost in the stars.

It was in the third week of my voluntary imprisonment in that house, for by then I rarely left it for exercise or other purposes, that I began to see, dimly at first, but with growing clarity, the host of astral organisms that haunted the Tower and seemed to emanate from it as though its presence gave them link or contact with the world of matter. They took form identical with that of the cherubim and seraphim of the familiar old prints, and soon I could discern them by day as well as night, filmy but distinct, circling about the Tower, and writhing tenuously in the air currents, sometimes descending into the busy twentieth-century street to mingle with the work-a-day crowds, potent, vital, but all unseen as they moved in weird co-existence with the grosser clay. By daylight, I was aware of distant, effulgent beings borne on bright pinions at an immense height near the crest of the Tower, which was the sun; but in the

57

hours of darkness these disappeared, and from out of the earth, where its base now formed a dense pit or pool of shadow engulfing the houses and the feeble lamps, came horrid, reptilian things of gargantuan proportions, which crawled sluggishly about the highways and leered with hydra-heads into the windows of drinking places, and upon groups of degenerates lounging enviously outside. Mostly, however, I was absorbed in watching the throng of evilly alluring entities in the likeness of men and women that seemed most closely connected with those humans within my range of vision. Unaware though he or she might be of their proximity, each person who entered the strange pageant was shadowed by two or three of these beings, fighting among themselves for possession of the body they pursued, and succeeding in proportion to the victim's natural inclination towards the debaucheries they sought, as by proxy, to enjoy.

For my part, I would recline at my window drinking whisky with an immunity at which I myself marvelled and speculating cynically on the moral lessons I witnessed. But my cynicism was shortlived, and swiftly on its heels came the birth of that fundamental horror which can never leave me again—the final enfoldment of my new gift.

I was crouching, one vivid afternoon, at my usual post, watching through the chink of the blind a veritable flock of ghoulish wraiths whirling about a young girl who stood on the kerb, wearing on her face a look of desperation that spoke of private tragedy. All the bitterness of some shocking disillusionment was in that look, and I noticed several people staring at her as they passed. She seemed torn between two impulses, and would first take a step forward as if to go upon her way, then halt again in indecision. And all the while the spirit creatures whirled faster about—beckoning.

I was callously wondering what they wanted of her when the end came. She uttered a ghastly, sobbing scream, and hurled herself with a kind of boneless wriggle under the wheels of a lorry.

I swung round, startled at a chorus of low-pitched, but intensely dreadful, laughter from behind me.

It is strange that, while unconcernedly watching the hounding of my fellows by these frightful Things, it had never occurred to me that I was other than a spectator. Now, at last, my eyes were fully opened, and I knew myself to be the destined plaything of a tribe of unthinkable horrors that confronted me. And, now, too, the understanding of my sensation of panic on first visiting the Tower became clear.

Fore-ordained, for what forgotten guilt I knew not—this dreadful fate had been awaiting me. My whole previous life had been no more than a cruel prelude to this ultimate moment—to know myself, in common with the greater portion of condemned Humanity, inevitably given over to the punishment for Original Sin. To be the sport of devils for ever and ever!

I grasped a new bottle of whisky from the table and drank myself into a state of insensibility.

They took me away at last after many weeks to the place where I am now kept. They thought, because I did not argue or seek to explain, that my mind had gone. As though any explanation could be made to ordinary folk without actually strengthening that belief! They supposed that I could not understand because I paid no attention when they spoke in my hearing of a legacy which was to be handled by trustees to provide for me until I regained my sanity, and of an asylum for dipsomaniacs to which I must go. They did not realise that I heard and understood every word, because I did not even bother to ask the source or size of my legacy. What could I care about this belated affluence when my mind was tortured by the new and appalling burden of knowledge thrust upon it?

I made no resistance when they took my few belongings and escorted me down to a waiting car, on the roof of which crouched an undraped huddle of gesticulating devils, and in the headlights of which a twenty-foot coil of a sluggish reptile was undulating.

I was glad to go when I heard that our destination was many miles away on the other coast, for I hoped against hope that, when I could no longer see the Tower, I might find forgetfulness. It was the vainest hope I could have held. I was drugged that night, and knew nothing of my journey to the West till I awoke at high noon in the room allotted to me at the asylum. It was an East-facing room, and they had wheeled my bed into a great bay-window where I could benefit by the sunshine and the healthy moorland winds.

I turned my head with lethargy, and looked broodingly out over the heather-clad expanse. The sky was cloudless—a vast vault of blue divided into two parts by a thin, yellow ray stretching vertically from horizon to zenith.

Came a movement from somewhere behind me, and a woman's voice asked, 'How do you feel?' I would have replied, for I still retain the instinct of politeness despite my absorption in matters that dwarf conversation; but it was at that very moment that I realised the meaning of the yellow ray. It was The Tower of Moab—so tall that no horizon can hide it—the fearful link forged in Man's defiance of God's ordaining, that has not only made contact with the higher realms, but given lease to the beasts of the Pit.

For the first time in my adult life I opened my lips and screamed.

THE CHILD

BECAUSE I AM not a member of the Psychic Research Society, and because I have never attempted to write a work of reference on occult subjects, I do not arrogate to myself any claim as an authority on such matters. Therefore I shall not put forward a so-called scientific explanation of my experience at Wailing Dip, preferring to leave this task to anyone clever enough to recognise the place from my account. Its real name, of course, is different.

Naturally I've read a mint of other people's efforts—both serious textbooks and works of fiction—but in spite of all the mass of conjectures about spirit manifestation which they have contained I am left guessing as to whether what I encountered in that revolting house was a spirit craving incarnation and angered by cruelly thwarted desire or some monstrous survival, if anything more horrifying still.

I got let in for the business entirely through my own curiosity, having always been keen on tales of the supernatural. I happened to be making a trip on my motor cycle to spend a couple of weeks with an old school friend on the other side of England, and, having plenty of time to spare, was amusing myself side-tracking from the main road wherever the countryside looked most attractive, in the hope of discovering some of those really old-world villages that one may still occasionally unearth in these days of the charabanc and filling station. Wailing Dip—its real name is equally quaint—proved to be one of these, and so charmingly unspoilt that I suppose I should have eventually paid it a lengthy visit even if my machine had not elected to break down badly just as I arrived. As it was, I found that it would be quite two days before the nearest garage could get spares from London and have me ready for the road again; and as I was still far from my destination I decided to stop and supervise the job. I accordingly wired my friend that I was hung up and went to arrange accommodation at the village inn. The latter was in every way in keeping with the place itself, a dear little, half-timbered cottage, with delightful rose-gardens at the back, extending to the borders of a dense wood. The landlady, an old-fashioned, motherly sort, who told me she had been running the place with the help of her two daughters since her husband's death six years before, made no difficulty about giving me a bed; and it was not long before I had collected my bag from the carrier of the motor cycle, washed my hands and face over the sink in the back kitchen, and taken a pint of beer out to a little table in the garden, where I relaxed myself to that particularly keen enjoyment which only a summer evening in the heart of the country can give.

Mrs. Jackson, as I will call the landlady, came out about half an hour later to see if I wanted any more ale, and, her daughters apparently being able to cope with whatever business was in the tap-room, stayed talking for some little while. After I had told her a few things about myself, where I was bound for, and how I came to be passing through the village, I remarked on my appreciation of a place so wonderfully restful and off the beaten track, and began to question her about the locality.

'Seeing that the spares I'm held up for can hardly get here before tomorrow evening,' I said, 'I should like to spend the day exploring the neighbourhood. Perhaps you can advise me if there are any places of special interest that I ought to see?'

She mentioned one or two old churches within a five-mile radius in addition to Gormingley Park, the seat of the local County family.

She feared, however, that I would not be able to look over the last-named place, since the family were in residence. They were, she explained, the chief landowners of the district, Wailing Dip itself being all part of the property.

'The Squire's one of the best,' she added. 'Old fashioned, like the village. He's never yet turned out a tenant who couldn't pay his rent so long as it was really a case of hard luck or illness. And as for trespassing, why the village folk can come and go as they like on his estate, outside the gardens, of course, and he'd never summons 'em—not unless they're poaching.'

'Well,' I replied, 'if that's the case I think I'll spend an hour or two at least rambling in that wood. It looks beautiful and no distance to walk.'

As Mrs. Jackson made no reply I turned to look at her, and found to my surprise that she was staring at me with an expression of the utmost concern. 'Don't go in that wood, sir,' she said, almost in a whisper, 'there are plenty of others as pretty.'

'But, Good Lord!' I explained, 'what's the matter with the place?' for I could read positive fear in her eyes. Then I added, for the sake of saying something: 'It's an old-fashioned district, but surely you don't date back to dragons?'

'There you go, sir!' she retorted almost angrily, 'laughing at everything before you even know what it is—just like the present generation.' Then, realising that I might be offended, for, after all, she'd only known me an hour, she went on with rather a forced smile: 'You young gentlemen from the big cities today don't believe in anything you can't see and touch, so I'm not going to say any more; but, speaking for meself, I wouldn't go in that wood alone for a thousand pounds, and if you want to laugh, sir, you may—but I still won't go!'

I was intrigued. This smelt like something really worth

investigating.

'Mrs. Jackson,' I said, 'because I arrive in this village on a motor cycle, a form of transport I detest, but can afford, don't class me with the type that carries a leggy flapper on the pillion and sports a cigarette holder a yard long. Believe me, I have really quite a serious mind. I have never seen a ghost, but would like to. I certainly don't laugh at them. You obviously have a good story to tell. Now, be an equally good soul, get me another tankard, bring yourself just what you feel like, and spare a bit more time to tell it.'

I had to say a lot more to convince her of my earnestness, but eventually elicited an unpleasant piece of local history which would have been interesting enough even without a sequel.

It appeared that, situated near the middle of the wood, which was a hundred acres in extent and very dense, there was a gamekeeper's cottage which had been inhabited by the same family in the Squire's employ for an indefinite period, the job of safeguarding that particular covert having passed from father to son for several generations. The last gamekeeper, however, had never had any children, and, on his death, only seven years ago, a north countryman and his wife had been taken on to fill the vacancy. The man, according to Mrs. Jackson, had been quite a decent sort, if just a bit morose and unwilling to mix with the village people, but his wife, though good-looking, had aroused an antagonism soon amounting to hatred from the first moment she appeared. She was extremely selfish and greedy for money, and seemed to derive no pleasure from looking after the cottage for her husband, with whom, it was said, she continually had the most frightful scenes. Unlike him, she was not averse to the society of her fellow creatures, nor was she above coming into the inn unescorted and drinking gin copiously with any poacher or passing tramp who would join her. At these times when her tongue was loosened she made no secret of her opinions as to the dead and alive character of the village, the shamefully humble nature of her husband's work, and the even more shameful smallness of his wages. Some of the older women in the village had tried to reason with her, pointing out that many others were satisfied with similar occupations on the Squire's land, and found their men's pay ample to bring up a happy family into the bargain, to which she flashed out that she wanted no squalling brat to guzzle the money that was already insufficient for two. Presently, however, the word went round, as such things will in a small community, that she was undoubtedly going to have a baby, and many were the hopes expressed that its advent would soften her and bring out the good which must be somewhere in her nature. In due time the child was stillborn, and buried a few days later near the village church-yard, the father alone attending the funeral. When the wife was able to be about again it was at once seen that no good had come of her experience.

Rather she was more slovenly and discontented than ever, and began to pay more frequent visits to the tap-room. Some pitied her, putting down her behaviour to the sense of fruitless travail. Others swore, by her own former statement, that she was glad to have no extra mouth to feed. A few hinted that the child had not been still-born.

The following year she brought another one into the world with the help of an old midwife who had attended all the births in the village for half a century, but who had not been called in the first time. It lived a fortnight and was found by its father, suffocated in its cradle, the day after the old cottager had gone back to her home. The wife said that she had been out in the wood for an hour chopping sticks, and that the baby must have turned over in its sleep.

The third year there came another, and this, too, met with an untimely end, being found with its neck broken on the floor beneath the cradle, which stood on a comparatively high trestle table, to be, as the mother explained, less easy for the cat to reach.

By this time everybody was talking—which, considering the woman's reputation, was not surprising—and when, the following year, a fourth tragedy took place, the two months' child this time having no marks to indicate the cause of death, an inquest was held by the express order of the Squire. The post-mortem revealed that some sharp, thin instrument, such as a hatpin, had been passed through one of the ear-drums into the brain, and that traces of any external bleeding must have been carefully washed away after the flow had ceased.

A verdict of wilful murder was recorded against the mother, and the case passed on to the next Assizes, where she was found 'guilty but insane', and sent to an asylum. Her husband then threw up his job and left the neighbourhood, and the village concluded that the terrible drama it had witnessed was at an end. There was, however, one more act to come.

Several months later the woman made her escape, and though the asylum authorities tried to keep it dark while attempting her recapture, the fact leaked out owing to her being seen by a courting couple entering the wood at Wailing Dip. Suspecting what had happened, these young people notified the village constable, who, through his County Station, confirmed the escape. He also learned that the convicted murderess who, it must be remembered, had not committed her crime until her last-born was two months old, was once more an expectant mother.

A search party was formed, and had already spent some hours beating the side of the wood adjacent to the village when word came through that the fugitive had been seen emerging on the far side and making her way towards a desolate stretch of moorland known as the Great Waste. Further scouring of the wood was thereupon called off, and those of the search party who were willing to continue their services were taken round to the new starting-point in police cars.

To cut a long story short, the mad woman was never captured. She had had nearly two hours' start from the time she left the wood owing to the fact that her second witness, not knowing of the hue and cry, had failed to report seeing her leave it.

With the assistance of bloodhounds she was traced to the edge of one of the abysmally deep pot-holes which dot the moor in that region. Failure to pick up the scent from that point was proof enough that she had either jumped or fallen into the abyss, and there the matter had to rest after a few half-hearted attempts to descend with ropes and lanterns.

'But ever since then,' Mrs. Jackson concluded, 'the feeling has grown around here that the wood and the cottage are haunted; and I doubt if a solitary soul has stepped inside its boundaries these two years excepting one poacher from a hamlet twenty miles away, who went there after pheasants and came in to me for the stiffest drink I'd got—that scared he couldn't, or wouldn't, tell exactly what he'd seen.'

'But,' I said, 'doesn't he sometimes shoot over it?'

Mrs. Jackson shook her head.

'Since that night, sir, there's never been a game bird in the whole covert. Never a fox. Never even a badger, as far as I know. You could stop with me a twelve month, and you'd never hear the cry of one, night or day. Plenty in the other woods—but not this side of the house. Besides...' she dropped her tone to a whisper... 'It's not only what doesn't live in the wood, sir. It's the poultry and things that's killed and taken away from the village, sir, by something that comes out of the wood, so people say!'

'But, Good God!' I ejaculated, 'what do they think it is that haunts the wood? Your story's horrible enough in all conscience without the final touch about stolen chickens, which are most likely taken by foxes; but has anyone ever seen a ghost there? If so, what's it like? Is it the mad woman herself or the poor little wretches she destroyed? Surely they would excite more pity than fear.'

Mrs. Jackson looked at me fixedly for a long, long moment before she answered; and twice I thought she was about to speak, and twice she failed. Then, at last: 'I have seen nothing, sir, and I don't think there is another woman or man in the village who *has,* because we have never stepped through the fence since that night she died. It is just the way we feel, and, as I have told you, sir, I for my part will not—not for *ten* thousand pounds.'

'But the poacher?' I cried out. 'The man from twenty miles away who was after pheasants?'

Once more she looked at me fixedly in the same compelling silence.

'He died, sir, within the month, of drink and delirium, shouting out the words he first uttered when he staggered into my kitchen long after I had closed the bar: "The Child! O God! The *horrible* Child!"'

As may be imagined, this revolting story did more than fire my imagination for a ghost hunt. So graphically had Mrs. Jackson told it, and in so obviously certain was she in her own mind that some dreadful curse or haunting had been left in the wood, that I found myself visualising the murder or murders with uncomfortable clarity, and although I enjoyed the excellently cooked supper which I later consumed in a cosy, lamp-lit parlour, I quite failed to derive the anticipated comfort from my night's rest in a little lean-to room which I had at first much admired, notwithstanding the old-fashioned luxury of a feather bed. My window, for one thing, looked out upon the wood, and I must confess that my brain persisted in speculating on what I should encounter there the next day—for I had determined to reconnoitre it when full daylight should give me confidence. Towards morning I slept a little, my rest broken by half-waking dreams of weird formless things watching my window from the gloom of the thicket.

I rose early and breakfasted well, telling Mrs. Jackson that one o'clock would suit me admirably for lunch. Then, carefully leaving my cap behind—for I knew that she would otherwise ask my destination and try to dissuade me—I strolled out, ostensibly to admire the garden. Once there, I quickly got out of sight among the pergolas, and was soon through the wire fencing.

My first action after progressing some yards among the trees was to produce my pen-knife and cut a stout branch from an ash sapling which I trimmed to a length of three feet. This imparted a measure of comfort, and would be useful for poking into hollow trunks or killing possible adders—for one half of me never expected results in the ghost-hunt, and sought to treat the expedition as a nature-study ramble. The thickness of the undergrowth amazed me, since the upper foliage was extremely luxuriant, and I had noticed in other woods that such a condition usually killed off ground vegetation through lack of sun. Here, apparently, the soil, some kind of dark loam, was sufficiently fertile to counteract this tendency, so that, what with trailing brambles and wild briars and thick curtains of creepers falling from higher branches, progress was really hard.

I remember thinking, too, that it was for the same reason quite the gloomiest wood I had seen, a place of perpetual twilight even in this glorious June weather. I had made up my mind to seek out the cottage first, and then, if it revealed nothing of interest, to spend the rest of the morning idling about after insects and wild-flowers. So, remembering that it was near the centre of the wood, I endeavoured to keep a course at right-angles to the border from the point of entry, no easy matter in so tangled a thicket. At last, however, I burst through a screen of dead brushwood into a kind of leafy tunnel, much overgrown but clearly a path. Just to my right another track branched off on the opposite side, roughly in the direction I had been following, and after a moment's thought I took to it, beating the brambles aside with my stick as I went along.

All this time, but for the occasional clatter of a wood-pigeon taking flight forty feet overhead, I realised that I had been progressing in a most uncanny silence. There had been no bird song, no scuttling of rabbits or rats, and never a sign of a squirrel. The fact dawned on me queerly, and I began to look round more carefully for traces of wild life. There were, I observed, plenty of *old* nests in the bushes, and I had already stumbled in more than one rabbit hole, but whether any rabbits slept in the warrens underground or whether they had been killed or driven out by fear of the Unknown Thing at which Mrs. Jackson had hinted, I could not guess. Despite the warmth I shivered and tramped on along the winding path. Then, round a sharp bend, I was suddenly confronted by the cottage: a grey, stone building, slate-roofed, and almost buried in a mass of ivy. Unlike most of those deserted dwellings, its windows were intact though, of course, uncurtained, and the fact that the front-door stood wide open, mute testimony to that last gamekeeper's state of mind when he took away his sticks of furniture, almost lent the place an air of immediate habitation. The cottage was much larger than I had expected, having two storeys, and I stood gazing at it for quite a minute before approaching further. Then, acting on some impulse of caution that I have never quite defined, I removed my shoes, and stole in absolute silence across the small clearing until I stood on the front step peering into the cobwebby little hall. The benefit I might have expected from the break in the trees forming the dwelling site was negated by the obvious fact that the fine spell was at an end; for during my short journey the sky had become obscured by thunder-clouds, so that the interior of the house was no lighter than the thicket through which I had come. But for this, I might have seen the baby handprints in the dust before I heard the cry.

As it was, the sound reached me first, and I stiffened against the lintel in sheer astonishment.

'Da, Da, Da,' came clearly in a childish treble from somewhere upstairs, accompanied by the rhythmic thumping of some hard object on the bare boards.

I stood absolutely petrified. It was so unmistakably the babble of a very young child that has not yet learnt to speak, and yet Mrs. Jackson had said definitely that no one lived in the place or, indeed, would venture near it. Still, someone must obviously be residing here unknown to the village; and I was about to announce myself with a 'Hello, there!' when I realised that, if so, they must be purposely in hiding—perhaps from the Law—and closed my lips. It was then that I glanced down and saw the little handmarks in the dust on the red tiles. They made definite tracks in all directions, crossing and re-crossing each other, many of them partially smudged out where the baby's knees had followed, as it had evidently crawled on all fours. Some traversed the step on which I was standing, indicating that it had been outside the cottage as well—and quite recently too, for there was not a speck of dust on these more clearly visible impressions. It struck me then, with a shudder for which I could not quite account, since the matter was more odd than terrifying, that every single imprint I could see had been made by the child itself. Nowhere was there the least sign of an adult footprint, and yet such thick dust must have lain many days—I could have believed months—since the last sweeping.

I frowned thoughtfully, and began tiptoeing across the flags to the foot of the stairs. After all, I was not going back at this point without solving the mystery, and if these queer people were, as they must be, fugitives from justice, they could not prosecute me for trespass, whilst, should they prove aggressive, I still had my ash plant and a strong arm. By this time the great storm which had gathered so speedily since I set out began to break, and, after a preliminary flash and distant rumble of thunder, a deluge of rain poured out of the sulphurous skies, its impact on the surrounding trees making a sullen, monotonous roar above which I could still faintly hear the thumps of the child playing in the upstairs room, and its shrill 'Da, Da, Da'.

My own muffled footfalls were quite inaudible, and so, hastening them, I stood a few seconds later on the almost pitch dark landing outside the hall open door of the room from which the noise was coming. There was more light inside the room than in the hall below, the surrounding trees on that side of the house being somewhat stunted, and I could see quite distinctly the half that was visible through the doorway. Like the rest of the place, it was totally unfurnished; but close against the wall to the right I noticed with astonishment a tumbled heap of carcasses of what appeared to be hens, rabbits and other small creatures furred or feathered, some just white skeletons, but others more or less lately killed and strangely gashed and mutilated. A disgusting odour of rottenness emanated from the heap and the floorboards all around seemed to be streaked with great gouts of blood.

I think it was at this juncture that I felt my first thrill of real horror as I asked myself into what hell hole I had wandered where a little child played among the putrid bodies of birds and beasts, and there was still no sign of parent or nurse, depraved beyond all measure though such a person must be.

But the sight that met me as I at last nerved myself to peer furtively through the crack of the hinge was the most weirdly unbelievable of all. Seated in the middle of the floor with its back to me was the naked figure of a baby of, perhaps, two years, prattling wordlessly in its sing-song treble as it played with a pile of gleaming white objects arranged about it in a circle. One of these, a globular thing of peculiar configuration, it grasped in its right hand, and banged down noisily among the rest. Opposite, just discernible in the shadowy corner, sat the largest brindled cat I had ever seen, dreamily watching the play through half closed, flame-yellow eyes. I suppose it must have been many minutes that I stood there dumbfounded, staring at this incredible spectacle, before my dazed senses registered its full hideousness, and then a strangled gasp escaped me, for I saw that the toy in the child's hand was a tiny human skull and that all the other white things were the various bones of an infant skeleton!

Slight as it had been, my involuntary intake of breath broke the spell that had enfolded that dreadful room. With a hellish scream, the cat leapt to the open door, glared at me in bestial rage, and bounded past me down the stairs, whilst the child dropped the skull and sprang with almost equal agility to the heap of rotting carcasses. There it paused, and, with no further sign of panic, slowly turned its face to mine.

That was not only the most ghastly moment of my life, but the most Faith killing. I would not have believed it possible for such stark fear to engulf a human mind without destroying it. One can vis-ualise the malignant expression of a brute desperado who never knew care or kindness making his last stand for life. One can picture him equally unleashing all his lust, malice and cruelty on defenceless women in time of revolution. And one only looks at him with anger and loathing, tempered, if one is very, very just, by pity that his loving child soul was crushed before it could develop. Somehow one always knows—pretty fancies apart—that he was once a child, loving, and asking love.

This Thing that confronted me in that place of death was spawn of hell—a foul thing, the greatest contradiction of Faith that human eyes have ever beheld! It had the body of a child, and the expression of the most frightful fiend. As I watched, petrified with terror, these thoughts tumbling tumultuously through my brain, I saw its malig-nant eyes light up with an unholy inner glow of triumph, and I saw one of its miniature hands delve down into the carcasses and come back bloody and holding a filthy old common kitchen knife. It gave a little babyish chuckle, infinitely horrible, and began to crawl towards me, and in the same moment I knew by some strange sense without daring to look away that the great cat was creeping stealthily up the stairs behind me, its head swinging from side to side, and its baleful yellow orbs fixed with dreadful purpose on the back of my head.

Shrieking like a frightened beast, I sprang backwards, twisting in the air as I went, and the next thing I can remember is running on and on in the drenching rain down one of the forest paths, whipping my face to ribbons on the thorns and nearly bursting my tortured lungs.

They told me when I was better that I said nothing understandable during my period of delirium, for which I was glad. As I stated at the commencement, I do not know if what I saw was a spirit or an unthinkable survival—that of the fifth child, born as the woman passed through the wood on her way to death on the moor. After all, chickens feed themselves from the moment of hatching.

The fact to be remembered is, however, that I will not divulge the real name of the place, for if I did, I should somehow be compelled to join another search party—and I *could not bear to look at the child again.*

THE DIRK

TRANTER'S MOOD as he turned in at the gate of 'The Spinney' on a certain early June evening is best described as one of very slightly qualified exultation. A private income, which he estimated at about £2,500 a year, for the rest of his life. No more sweating at uncongenial jobs under the galling dictatorship of employers. No more penurious interludes in slum lodgings harried by the constant fear of meeting creditors. Above all, this delightful country home in a corner of England unspoilt by the suburban builder, with its peaceful lovely gardens where he could indulge his poetic side in interminable waking dreams. And all achieved by one bold, well-planned stroke— the work of a single night.

The gravel of the drive crunched familiarly as he strode up to the house between banks of flowering shrubs; and tendrils of creeper swaying here and there from the weathered brickwork as the evening breeze caught them up seemed to wave a welcome to the place he had known and loved in boyhood. Always a haven, the old house still drowsed on, oblivious to the march of industry and growth of cities—an old-world refuge of magic memories unbroken, surely, in their tenor of peace, but for that one night six months ago.

And that, thought Tranter, as another picture sprang into his mind, must be outweighed by the older associations. He shrugged, then straightened his back, and fumbled for the key. This was no time to ponder an isolated flaw in the serene history of his inheritance.

But ponder it he must, for control of the muscles is easier than control of thought, and despite his will a second picture kept super-imposing itself upon the scene before him—the picture of the same house, not softly golden in slanting sun-rays, but blackly outlined against a December night sky, its windows dimly lighted from within, and the dead body of his brother drooping over the sill of one that stood open to the rain and wind. Oh well, if this one memory of all would persist, better to meet it and reconstruct the whole thing in his imagination as he had done a hundred times since, but, this time, in the actual setting of the event. Then his sense of proportion could re-assert itself and relegate it to its proper place as the briefest episode in his long association with the house, and therefore the least deserving of recollection.

He was not surprised by the darkness and the faintly musty smell when he opened the front-door, for the building had been closed and shuttered for nearly half a year, but he frowned at the thin veil of dust on the switch-board as he snapped on the lights. Somehow he had expected there would be no pollution so far from the abomination of factories and arterial roads.

Not stopping to remove his hat or raincoat, Tranter made straight for the door on his left which opened into what had been his brother's study. Here too he switched on the lights and glanced alertly about him. Everything was as he last remembered it, a tribute to the thoroughness of the detective officers on completion of their search for clues. He walked over to the shuttered window and bent down. Someone had carefully cleansed the woodwork where the stain had been. There was nothing to remind him unpleasantly of the murder— only that wretchedly insistent mental image that would obtrude itself. Well, it was a pity that violence had been necessary, but it was fair. John had had all the enjoyment of the house and the money for years, whilst the younger brother had been fobbed off at their father's death with a beggarly £5,000—enough, as the will had suggested, to set him up for life if judiciously invested in a business of his own. The younger brother glanced again at the window-sill and smiled wryly. Now it was his turn. He had never had, as he understood things, a business type of mind, and the legacy would not have brought in a living income from public investments. He had been too wise to 'blue' it, but he had tried to double it—by the time-honoured methods—and when it had all vanished his brother had not only refused to help him, but had taken it upon himself to censure him.

That had been the real trouble with John. He had been practical to the point of stolidity, had lacked all sympathy with artistic souls, and could not understand their incapacity to compete in the cheating and haggling of commercial life. Why, he had been so infernally unromantic that he would have been just as happy in some damned suburb doing what he considered his duty, had their positions been reversed.

The present heir was better fitted to bestow upon 'The Spinney' the appreciation it deserved. The present. heir! It was fortunate that their father, in his desire that the line should continue, had so framed his will as to embrace the possible succession of the younger son, but it had forced the issue when John became engaged.

Tranter felt for and lit a cigarette. He had already gone far in that mental readjustment to accomplish which he had planned the visit prior to the arrival of his domestic staff. The crime—he clicked his tongue at the word—had been brilliantly simple in execution, neither over-elaborate, nor bunglingly amateurish. There lay the advantage of the imaginative temperament. He had motored from London with false number-plates salved from a scrap-dealer's yard, on a night when he knew that visitors would be unlikely, parked his car on the edge of an adjacent common, and walked to the house in a pair of shoes, which, having never previously worn, he was not known to possess. Crossing the lawn, he had tapped on the study window and been recognised by his brother, who was alone. John had let him in by this unorthodox way of ingress at the urgent plea of secrecy, in all probability supposing him engaged in some escapade prejudicial to the family name, and he had then unobtrusively worked his way to the door while making conversation about an imaginary road accident.

This part of the picture became peculiarly vivid as Tranter stood musing by the writing-desk. He could almost see his brother standing on the hearth-rug as he had stood nearly seven months before, barking brief interruptions to his narrative in his usual, unfriendly fashion.

He moved over and slipped nonchalantly in front of the door as he had done on that former occasion, and recalled how he had noiselessly turned the key behind him, thanking his stars the lock was oiled.

And he visualised anew his studiedly careless stroll across to the fireplace, saying as he crossed the room: 'But, damn it, man, if you won't let me stay the night, at least lend me the fare to Town.'

Then whipping the Highland dirk from its sheath above the mantel and driving it into his brother's body.

Yes, that part *was* vivid. He could see the stupid, blank look that spread over John's face, to be succeeded by one of hate as he lurched towards him. He could feel the muscles of his legs grow tense as they had grown that night when he sprang away—not in fear, for he saw that John had no more than seconds to live—but to avoid the blood. And what a prodigous leap had carried him over the sill before his brother had time to stumble there and collapse!

He remembered just how he had withdrawn John's pocket-book to supply the evidence of motive and had abstracted a wad of notes, deliberately allowing a few to fall with the empty wallet to give an impression of panic which, curiously, he had not actually felt. Then the swift flight back to the car with John's dying whisper in his ears: 'You skunk! I'll get you for this!' As though the fool had not realised his wound was mortal. Tranter had not met a soul until he was back on the main road, where his car—of a popular make and colour—would attract no special attention; and he had taken the precaution of making a leisurely detour so as to approach London from the opposite side. At a convenient point *en route* he had again deviated from the main road and consigned his false plates and shoes to a pond, replacing them with the originals, which had been concealed in the tool-locker. A more painful precaution on arrival at his flat in Wells Street had been the burning of the stolen notes—a wise one, though, for the police had subsequently stated that some of their numbers were recorded on the last counterfoil of the dead man's cheque-book. Tranter, as next-of-kin, had attended the inquest, been formally interrogated as to his own movements on the night of the murder, and satisfied the coroner with a fictitious account of a visit to a girl who was an artist's model and lived near Folkestone—an alibi supported by the girl herself—not without an eye to the future.

The police remarked on the absence of fingerprints—Tranter had worn gloves—and the jury brought in a verdict of 'Murder by some person or persons unknown'. Now he was about to enter upon his inheritance.

Once more his eyes roved round the familiar furnishings and sought the spot on the wall where the dirk had hung. It was the only object, apparently, which had been moved from its customary place—probably consigned to Scotland Yard's museum. It would be amusing to ask for it back and restore it to its old place, and kill the impression that it had ever been used for other than ornamental purposes. Tranter crushed his cigarette in an ash-tray and walked slowly across to the empty hearth. There would be a cheerful fire in it the following night when, after the wedding arranged to satisfy local susceptibilities, he and Vera moved into their new domain. Incidentally, she should be along at any moment now, having promised to walk up from her rooms in the village where she was staying in preparation for the ceremony.

Tranter heaved a big sigh of satisfaction and leaned with his elbows on the mantel shelf. At least he was as fond of the girl as he had been of any and the main point was that all this property was now his without dispute, unless he took into account his brother's futile threat to 'get him'—whatever he may have meant by that.

Perhaps John had believed in ghosts and their power to inspire fear, but if his spirit really *could* return, it would soon tire of haunting when it found its efforts ignored. Tranter was unconvinced as to the existence of ghosts and their ability to appear to the living; he was materialist enough to fear nothing which lacked physical form, and was prepared to listen with equanimity to any traditional moaning or chain-rattling which the departed could produce.

He smiled at his reflection in the mirror above the mantelpiece, and, with the conceit common to the egocentric, fell to studying the cast of his features. He would make a fitting owner for 'The Spinney', with his straight brows, aristocratic nose, and square, clean-shaven chin.

He took off his hat and smoothed back the black, well-groomed hair from his temples. Yes. He was in his proper sphere!

He had been standing thus complacently for some minutes when his notice was drawn to an unfamiliar object in the background reflected in the mirror. It took the form of something small and oval with a bright centre, quite unlike anything he remembered seeing since he had entered the room. But what most held his attention was the fact that, instead of resting upon any of the numerous pieces of furniture behind him, it seemed to be poised in mid-air as though suspended from the ceiling by an invisible thread. He glanced round hastily to ascertain what it was, but, to his surprise, could see nothing whatever to correspond with the reflection. The object, whatever it was, should have been just in line from where he stood with the edge of a bookcase, at the end of the third row down. Stooping forward a little to intensify his vision he approached the bookcase. No. There was nothing there—not even an oval mark in the designs of the bindings. He squinted sideways trying to intercept some trick of light on the polished front of the shelf, but without result. 'Well, that's damned odd!' he muttered, going back to the fireplace.

As he neared the mirror he saw the reflection again, just as before.

'Must be a flaw in the glass,' he said aloud, 'or mildew behind the quicksilver.' He peered closely into the mirror, but could detect no flaw. As an afterthought he placed himself in front of the reflection, which immediately disappeared. It was there again when he took a pace to one side, and back he went to the bookcase. This time he picked up a rug and draped it over the entire row of shelves before returning to the hearth.

He also made the journey backwards, keeping his eyes fixed on the approximate situation of the illusory oval. It was not visible, from any point of his transit; but the mirror showed it again, when he turned to look, now rather more clearly defined owing to the plain background afforded by the rug. The impression that it was nothing to do with the bookcase, but actually hung at some point between it and the overmantel was, moreover, stronger than ever. Tranter set his teeth and stared at the reflected object. He had never given much serious thought to ghost-lore, but, if this were his righteous brother's idea of 'getting him', it would take more than meaningless hallucinations to scare him out of 'The Spinney'. Nonetheless, a very slight premonitory shiver ran down his spine.

'No,' he said more loudly than before, 'it must be something in the glass.' And then he remembered a powder-box of Vera's with a tiny mirror in the lid, which he had found in the car and slipped into his pocket. He sorted it out, opened it, and turned the reflector towards the bookcase. It was too small to give a comprehensive view, but, by holding it close to his face, he was able to see several square feet of the wall behind him at one time. He located the rug, which he had hung up, and, by turning the box in his hand, managed to cover the whole of its area systematically. There was no sign of the mysterious oval between it and himself.

With a sigh of relief, for his nerves had been keyed higher than he realised, he closed the box and involuntarily looked again for the deceptive image in the large looking-glass.

It was no longer there.

Tranter pulled the back of one hand across his forehead and brought it away wet. Were his eyes playing him tricks? Or was there really something uncanny about the room? He told himself that he was not frightened—just puzzled and interested. Yes—that was it—puzzled and interested. All the same, he shivered a second time, and cursed under his breath.

A fancied movement on his right caused him to glance quickly in that direction, and he spun round as though he had been shot.

Close behind him *on the other side of the room*, and gleaming like some malignant eye, he had seen the reflected oval—larger and brighter because of its apparent nearness, the shining centre now defined as a cleanly cut, elongated diamond.

But the room was void of anything additional to its normal fittings. There *was* no oval.

At that moment Tranter could not bring himself to look back into the glass. He had a sudden desire for the twilight of the garden. He took a quick step towards the door and cried out sharply.

Some unnoticed obstacle had come into violent contact with his left shin. The pain momentarily steadied him, and he stood rubbing the place for several seconds before he realised that there was nothing visible with which he could have collided. With trembling fingers he rolled down his stocking. The blue outline of a bruise was just perceptible. He dragged the stocking up again and half straightened his back. There was something furtive about his movements by now. His eyes travelled fearfully from side to side. He took another pace forward cringingly, as though expecting a blow, and met no obstruction. A second with equal success, and he broke into a run.

The next moment he had tripped over something unseen and crashed heavily on his face. He writhed over onto his side and cowered, half stunned, then scrambled to his knees with a whimper of fright, shying sideways as a sharp stabbing pain seared his right shoulder. He gaped foolishly at bright splashes of blood dripping down upon his hands. Some invisible horror out of empty air had slashed keenly through coat- and shirt-sleeve.

Suddenly, a panic, dwarfing all previous qualms, flooded his whole being. He dared not rise, but dug his fingers into the pile of the carpet, and attempted to crawl to the door, only to be met by a storm of painful stabs about the arms and shoulders—stabs that fell inconceivably out of the void. But that they were not imaginary the rents and blood on his coat testified.

He shrieked at the top of his voice, leaped up, and dashed frantically back towards the fireplace, away from the unseen force which seemed concentrated between him and escape. As he ran, his image rushed at him in the big looking glass—a wild, dishevelled figure with fear-maddened eyes and distorted features, chalk-white, hands upraised. *And behind it, darting through empty air, sped the gleaming oval.*

Immediately above his head it stopped and hung once more immobile.

Then, as he huddled shaking and sobbing against the mantelpiece, his stare set hypnotically upon the reflection aloft, it slowly changed its shape. The base of the oval grew downward until it resembled a pedestal, and the bright diamond extended upward inch by inch to form a tall triangle of polished steel bearing an engraved design.

And Tranter saw them at last as hilt and blade—the dirk which had killed his brother. No longer foreshortened in thrusting poise, but brandished upright like a warning of death, the weapon hung in space, its point dappled with fresh blood.

Even as his ears caught the sound of a footstep in the hall and the rattle of the door-handle, the image in the glass swept down and forward. He choked and fell into the hearth—blood pouring from his mouth.

The circumstances of Tranter's death naturally demanded an inquest, and the girl, Vera, was the first witness called. She testified to having gone to the house alone to keep an appointment with the deceased.

She had let herself in with a key, and, hearing a cry of evident pain or fear coming from the study, had hurriedly opened the door and discovered her fiancé lying face downward in the fireplace vomiting blood. She broke down at this point, and the coroner considerately allowed her to sit during the remainder of her evidence. He asked her as few questions as possible, and called the next witness as soon as she had described the rapid stiffening of the body, and her attempts to feel Tranter's pulse. The telephone being already installed in readiness for their occupation, she had been able to call up the police at once, and had awaited their arrival in the garden.

Henry Stirling West, Divisional Police Surgeon for the district, gave evidence of being called to the house to view the remains, which showed no sign of external injury. He had subsequently assisted at an autopsy carried out by Sir Bartlett Haviland, the Home Office expert, at which, on removing the dead man's clothes, they had found a bruise on the left breast corresponding with a protuberance of the fire-kerb, across which the body had fallen. This was confirmed by Sir Bartlett himself, the next witness, and the coroner asked him, 'What in your opinion, was the cause of death?', to which the specialist replied unhesitatingly: 'Rupture of the heart, due to falling heavily on the corner of a fire-kerb.'

'And there was no other sign of external injury?'

'None of any moment.'

'What do you think caused the fall?'

Sir Bartlett shrugged. 'It is impossible to say definitely. He may either have tripped or had an attack of giddiness. I am inclined to discount the latter, as all his organs were fit and healthy, and there was no trace of excess alcohol in the stomach.'

'Do you imagine he could have been struck down by an assailant?'

'There is no evidence pointing to that. The only marks on the skin were the bruise, already described, and another on the left shin which could also have been caused in the fall.'

A verdict of 'Death by misadventure' was finally recorded, but the coroner, an old friend of Sir Bartlett's, was tempted to re-open the subject when the latter was taking a glass of wine in his library, after the proceedings were closed.

'The Press,' he remarked musingly, 'have already made the most of certain coincidences, such as the violent ends of both Tranter and his brother, in the same room, and I can quite understand that you people must often find it judicious to suppress evidence that is not essential. Personally, I'm puzzled by a man of Tranter's youth and fitness falling, for no apparent reason, with such heaviness as to burst his heart. Did you draw any inferences not expressed in Court?'

Sir Bartlett stroked his chin with deliberation.

'Make what you like of it,' he answered at length, 'but treat this confidentially, as a man in my position cannot afford to suggest supernatural explanations publicly. Tranter's heart was not ruptured by the fall. Though there was no break in the skin of chest or back, a lobe of it had been cleanly severed as though by a sharp blade. You would produce the same phenomenon if it were possible to stab a man *from inside!* Another point for reflection,' he added, emptying his glass, 'is that the dirk with which the brother was killed has mysteriously disappeared from the Yard's collection of murder-weapons!'

THE CHORDS OF CHAOS

'HAVE YOU EVER heard of astral music?'

Rex Eustace replaced his pipe in his mouth, leaned back and looked at me interrogatively. We had just finished dinner, and were taking our coffee on the terrace in the cool of the evening.

It was not the first time that we had touched upon the supernatural. Many a night in our dug-out "over there", mutual interest had led our thoughts along the same path, the light of one flickering candle casting its elusive shadows on walls of damp earth, lending a spice of reality to the topic.

But back home in my friend's pretty, old-fashioned garden, with the dark uncertainties of war at an end, and a hundred trivialities of daily amusements to occupy our minds, I wondered what train of thought had prompted this sudden question.

'I'm not sure,' I replied cautiously. 'What exactly do you mean?'

'I mean music which belongs to the spirit-world and can be reproduced by a medium during a state of trance.'

'I have heard of that,' I said, 'but have never seen it done. Have you?'

'Yes. Quite recently,' he answered.

I became interested. Spiritualism is a subject of which I know little, but it is a fascinating study.

'I have a neighbour,' he continued, 'a Mr. Julian Westenhanger, who is a medium. He will sit down at the piano, make his mind a blank, and play the harmonies that come to him from beyond the barrier. The thing is absolutely genuine. He really plays the most wonderful stuff, quite unlike anything else which I have heard. Nearly sent me into a trance myself the other day, when I was listening to it. On regaining consciousness he can recall nothing. It's most weird.'

'I should like to hear him,' I said quietly.

'You will have the opportunity,' Eustace declared. 'He is well known as a musician, and has been asked to give an organ recital in St. Mary's Church tomorrow night after Evensong.'

'Yes. But I mean the spirit-music.'

My friend looked at me quizzically for a moment. Then his gaze travelled vacantly to the sky, as though he were considering some problem.

'I don't know him very well,' he observed at last, 'because he has only come to the place during the war, and I have been away, as we both know; but, if you really care to meet him, I see no reason why we should not drop in for an hour right away. What d'you think?'

'Certainly,' I responded, rising to my feet.

And with that one word I ignorantly committed myself to the most painful, ghastly, and grotesquely incredible adventure of my life—a thing made the more bizarre by its setting of peaceful security in the little country town.

Mr. Westenhanger was at home, and we were promptly shown into his drawing-room. I walked over towards the French windows and glanced casually about me. One can frequently read something of a man's character in the objects with which he surrounds himself. To my disappointment, however, this room presented no features of especial interest. In all respects it was commonplace. I do not mean drab, or ugly, but just average—the kind of reception-room one would find in a dozen small country houses. There were the usual rosewood chairs, the usual landscape pictures on a pale-blue wallpaper, a chintz-covered sofa, and various other pieces of strictly conventional furniture. A vase of lilies, standing on the piano, diffused a sweet though rather heavy perfume.

I began to regret that my friend had told me nothing of the man himself.

'At all events,' I thought, 'he is not a genius of the long-haired tribe'—a deduction which was verified as our host made his appearance.

In no way did Westenhanger give the impression of an artist except in his slender hands, with the long, sensitive fingers of the musician. Of medium height, with rather close-cropped hair, and neatly attired in a grey suit, he also fell very short of my ideal spiritualist.

Eustace rose, and said in a formal introduction: 'This is my friend Mr. Steer—one of the overseas crowd. He is staying with me for a week to celebrate peace.'

I bowed and extended my hand.

'You see,' I remarked, 'I am a great lover of music. That is why I asked Eustace to bring me round.'

For an instant a look of pleasure crossed his face, but, as his hand gripped mine, the expression seemed to change. What emotion it depicted, I am powerless to describe; but the effect upon me as I met his eyes was most peculiar. I experienced simultaneously a feeling of exultation and loathing, which vanished as swiftly as it had arisen.

You may think that, having heard of him as an occultist, I was unconsciously on the look-out for something abnormal, but I am not usually imaginative, and the queer sensation puzzled me. If I had given any sign, however, of what I felt bound to consider a ridiculous fancy, neither Eustace nor Westenhanger himself appeared to have noticed it. The latter leaned one elbow on the piano and courteously

91

motioned me to a chair.

'You play yourself, Mr. Steer?' he inquired. I was obliged to confess my claims were limited to admiring the performance of others, and the conversation drifted for a while over many diverse subjects.

Presently Westenhanger seated himself at the piano and began to play from memory. Some of the pieces were unfamiliar, and others the best-known triumphs of famous composers. The whole production was an aesthetic banquet, so faultless was his technique and so soulful the rendering. I was lost in the pleading accompaniment of Tosti's 'Parted' when he turned abruptly from the instrument.

'You will take a glass of port, won't you?' he said in the most matter-of-fact tone. It was more of a command than a question, and before either of us could reply, he had rung the bell. Brought back to reality by his sudden change of demeanour, I began to fear that we should be denied the real object of our visit, when Rex broke the silence.

'Steer, like myself, is interested in the supernatural,' he ventured, 'and I took the liberty of mentioning to him your mediumistic powers. I am sure he would like you to give us some astral music, if it will not trouble you too much.'

The way in which he spoke amused me slightly. It seemed by far too casual a tone for such a matter, and I felt a little apprehensive lest it should be taken as the irreverent banter of a sceptic.

Our host made no answer until the servant had placed a decanter with three glasses upon a side-table, and the door was once more closed.

I was becoming quite excited, like a schoolboy immersed in a blood-curdling ghost story, while he poured out the red wine and handed each of us a glass.

At last he turned towards me thoughtfully. 'It is a thing I very rarely do at anyone's request,' he affirmed. 'Do you really wish me to?'

'Yes,' I answered briefly.

'Very well. You shall hear it. But, remember, I have no idea what I am about to play, and shall remember nothing of it afterwards—so please ask me no questions.'

That was all, and there had been no great difficulty in persuading him. I took a sip of port, exchanged a glance with Eustace, and leaned forward to listen.

Once more Westenhanger took his place at the piano and, closing his eyes, let his head sink forward upon his breast. For the space of several minutes, there was absolute silence. He seemed instantly to have fallen asleep. Then his lean, white fingers began to wander over the ivories with a strange, half-conscious caress, and the first rippling notes of an unknown music rang out in the stillness.

Even with those first trembling bars I held my breath. It was as though a primeval voice were speaking out of the unborn darkness of Eternity. Without rhyme or rhythm, the sound rolled forth, now low and plaintive, now rising to an exultant crescendo, in waves of unearthly melody, alluring, though foreign to the human ear. To this day I wonder whether an instrument made by man could have produced those sounds, or whether, rendered receptive by some unseen influence, I heard them in spirit alone. Whatever their origin, to me they were real; and as I closed my eyes, the more readily to absorb their wild cadence, they conjured up vague, formless pictures, chasing each other across an opaque veil.

Astounding as it may seem, scarcely a moment could have elapsed since the medium had entered into his trance, but already I was forgetting time, place, everything, in a kind of hypnotic sleep. How long this condition lasted I do not know. The scented air seemed to grow denser and still more dense, a green mist surrounded me, and my ears were filled with a reverberating roar. Fainter and less distinct came those musical waves, and some dormant inner consciousness called into being a dream that was not a dream—the memory of a long-forgotten life.

I stood alone on the outskirts of a great multitude, thronged in the moonlit courtyard of a temple. On three sides rose massive walls of hewn stone, their castellated summits dimly outlined against the starry sky; and in front, the temple itself, a vast pile, wrought in black marble, with towering minarets, its base half hidden in a pool of inky shadow. There was something terrifying in its looming majesty—a callous, indestructible pride.

The brilliant moon immediately overhead poured down a cold, white light upon the sea of upturned faces, from which came the murmur of a thousand tongues. Each motionless figure was bare-headed, and clad in flowing robes of some dark material. My own dress was the same, a long purple garment, embroidered with serpents of black and gold, and fastened on the left shoulder with a single metal clasp.

I looked down at my feet. They were encased in sandals of raw hide; and, strangely enough, there seemed to me nothing unusual in this attire. It was as though I knew no other and had worn it all my days. My eyes lifted, and once more I gazed round the packed assembly.

All were waiting, even as I waited—but for what? Dimly I remembered that it was the performance of some mystic rite, but of its nature I was profoundly ignorant; nor was there a sign within the whole spectacle, save for a restless motion which now began to stir the feet of the crowd.

Presently I felt a hand upon my shoulder, and became aware of another standing by me, the clear light revealing his bearded face.

'Greeting to thee,' I whispered in a language long dead, though one which I spoke with natural ease.

'Greeting,' he answered softly; and, by some freak of double consciousness, I knew him for the past self of my friend Eustace. Evidently we have been age-long associates, and, in my dream memory, trusted comrades-in-arms even as in the present life. One bend in the eternal spiral of evolution, and the conditions were repeated.

'Tell me then,' I said, addressing him by his ancient name, though that I have now forgotten, 'to what ceremony are we bidden—thou and I?'

'It is the night of our father Chaos,' he replied, 'of him that bred the Earth in fine mist: yet of the manner of his worship I too am without knowledge. Once in ten score years this festival is held, nor is its nature told to any save to the priests alone; for some say that no man of the people shall leave these walls alive!'

At these words a chill crept over my body; a thrill of expectant fear and a sense of dread stirred my heart. With a shudder I turned to look behind me, and, as I did so, the mutter of voices grew in volume. There came the shuffle of many sandals upon stone, like waves on a shingle beach, and the mob surged outwards to the sides of the court, so that we were jostled this way and that.

With a resonant clang, two gates of bronze swung back, and as a lane opened through their midst a great cry went up to the echoing heights: 'They come! They come!'

Then stillness fell again as the babel of tongues gave place to the tramp of a marching column.

Through those twin gates they entered—a sinuous procession of white-robed priests, each bearing upon his brow a tiny lamp like a diadem of flame, and at their head strode a stately leader, his vestments glittering with a maze of jewels. As he went, those in the foremost ranks bowed themselves to the ground.

By reason of our stature, my companion and I were able to see him over the heads of the throng, and it was with an inward shock that I saw in him the soul of Julian Westenhanger—yet still I dreamed.

Speechless, the column moved on until it came to the temple steps, where it halted in a half-circle, the high-priest solemnly ascending until he stood within the gloom of the portal. Not another sound could be heard as, in a dirge-like chant, he addressed the tremendous gathering:

'Give ear, O people of Atlantis—ye that have come up from the four points of the heavens to make obeisance to the Father of Life. Ye are the dust, the fragments of his creation. How then shall ye exalt yourselves to tyrannize the world that gave you birth? Humble yourselves, things of vileness, that your Father may see in you repentance. Haste ye, slaves of vanity, to make your sacrifice; for Chaos, the Lawless, the Ungoverned, knoweth not delay.'

He ceased, and withdrew into the dark interior, followed by the file of priests, while, in echo of his words rolled up the muffled answer:

'We make our sacrifice.'

Little did they they guess by what means the Black Powers would take their toll.

One and all bowed themselves low, hushed and awestruck, awaiting manifestation yet untold.

It came.

A burst of thunderous music boomed through the columns of the temple, a volume of bass chords from some tremendous organ. Out of the inmost recesses it poured forth to fill the quivering air, until the whole huge fabric of the temple throbbed with its mighty utterance.

Its effect upon the audience was instant and notable. Some swayed dizzily as they stood, some fell upon their knees, while others prostrated themselves as though overcome.

For my own part, I felt that my reason was tottering. The mass of sound—it seemed almost tangible—hammered in my ear-drums with a sensation of acute physical pain; and all the time those stupendous notes increased in power until they broke and mingled in one terrific paean, flinging its echoes infinitely into space.

All about me the wonderful, unholy music pealed out, whirling in a tempest irresistible, and my senses withered like shrivelled grass. Dazed and half blind, I sought vainly for some pathway of escape, but the monstrous walls mocked me, and the crowd, a maelstrom of formless spectres to my distorted vision, pressed close around.

Then came the fearful climax.

Somewhere within that temple of sin the unseen instrument crashed into hideous discord, causing an anguish no human tongue could describe. My whole frame was racked with the agony of it, and the last shreds of self-control swept away in blind, brutal insanity.

Within one flash of time the court became a ghastly scene of carnage, men and women rending each other in frenzy of diabolic hate, and beating their own heads against the granite floor. In tortured fury I clawed and struck at my companion, snarling like a beast—my one passionate desire to kill—to kill! His arms gripped me with a superhuman strength, his teeth were grinding at my throat... and in that appalling moment I regained consciousness.

Eustace was crouched near to me upon the carpet, his eyes reflecting my own unutterable horror; and Westenhanger lay spread-eagled upon the keyboard, sunk in deep oblivion.

Mutely we staggered out into the twilight.

All night I lay awake, tired out in mind and body, hut unable to sleep for the poignant remembrance of that dreadful nightmare. Time after time my thoughts travelled back over every detail of the sinister drama which had become part of my waking life, until no vestige of doubt remained that it was true. Not a single word had Eustace exchanged with me upon the subject, for each knew what the other had seen.

Had we not stood together through the ordeal up to the consummation of all things—victims of the black magicians in old Atlantis? Both had awakened with the same loss of energy, the same indelible terror of the spirit, and, try as I would, I could not put aside the premonition that oppressed me.

The story was not complete. The curtain had yet to rise for the last act. And somewhere, locked in the fathomless heart of Nature, existed that foul combination of sound-waves which could turn the whole human race into a race of maniacs.

In the morning I felt no relief. My head ached, my limbs were heavy, and I was shadowed with uneasiness. Eustace noticed it, but himself looked thoroughly overwrought.

'It is the effect of last night,' he explained; but said no more. On that Sunday, nothing could restore our vitality or our contentment. We tried to read, to play bowls, even to weed the garden, but our listless melancholy only increased.

About five in the afternoon Rex found me in my room, staring out of the window, and appeared anxious to unburden himself of something.

'Are you coming with me to the evening service?' he inquired after a pause.

'If you wish me to,' I returned. I did not ask the name of the Church. It would be St. Mary's, I felt sure.

'Very well,' he said briefly; 'I will be ready in half an hour.'

At six we were in our places for the celebration of Evensong.

It was a fine building containing a great deal of beautiful carving, and some very noteworthy stained glass. The size, I thought, was sufficient to hold a congregation of about six hundred; and, to judge by the way the pews were filling, quite that number would be present, many, no doubt, having come more for the concluding organ recital than to join in the divine service.

The architecture of oaken roof-beams, the magnificent reredos and the stone columns, all occupied a large part of my attention. I am no great churchman, and always prefer a church when it is empty, from the artistic point of view.

Some time before the benediction I had found Westenhanger sitting in a front pew, just below the pulpit. To render the service short, no sermon was given, and I do not think I was the only one glad of this, as the time for his part drew near. Despite my recent awful experience at his house, the consequences of which I could not yet shake off, I found myself looking forward to a new exhibition of his skill.

At last the blessing was given, priest and choir were gone, and quietly Westenhanger left his seat.

It was noticeable that, of the whole congregation, not one man, woman, or child moved, and I could not help smiling as I remembered the words: 'A prophet is not without honour...'

And then came the greatest artistic treat I have ever known.

If this man could handle the piano, his execution on the richest of all instruments was nothing less than superb. Oblivious to my surroundings, I listened in ecstasy as he played from Mozart, Mendelssohn, and Elgar indiscriminately, each piece with more feeling, if possible, than the last.

But, suddenly, something took place which called me back to earth from the sublime. The key-note of his music was changing as he drifted on into a fresh composition. The seductive charm of his touch remained, but something cold had crept in, like the voice of a condemned soul; and as I listened to its evil grandeur, a frightful conviction stabbed through my heart. In a trance, or with the full consciousness of a hellish purpose, he was playing once more the music of my dream.

With a rush, that undefined fear which had hung over me, took form. Another moment, and the awful Chords of Chaos would hurl destruction upon hundreds of innocent victims. Panic-stricken, I turned to seek the help of Eustace. He had risen, and was standing motionless in the aisle. I tried to follow but a supernatural power had paralysed my limbs, so that I could only watch, wondering childishly what he would do. Then I saw that he held something in his right hand—something which glittered. A man behind me, in the next pew, had evidently seen it as well, for, with an inarticulate cry, he sprang forward.

It was too late.

There came a muffled report, a spurt of flame, and half-way through a bar the music stopped.

As the horrified congregation leaped to its feet, Julian Westen-hanger fell dead at the base of the organ.

There is little more to tell.

I cannot bear to linger upon the sad conclusion. The silent horror of the onlookers, the arrest, the trial, the verdict—all is a lurid dream of yesterday: for what Bishop, or what stern-faced jury, would hear this testimony and believe?

Among many of its kind, in the grassy churchyard of St. Mary's, stands a tombstone inscribed: 'JULIAN WESTENHANGER... REQUIESCAT IN PACE.'

In the northern shadow of the belfry, beyond the pale of consecrated ground, is a nameless grave. Some say it is that of one who desecrated the House of God by the Unforgivable Sin.

Let me pray that two souls find justice before a Higher Judge.

THE MEERSCHAUM PIPE

November 17th.

NEVER HAVING TRIED keeping a diary before, it will be amusing to see whether I have enough mental energy to go on with it. At all events my new-found leisure will not give me the excuse of being too busy. The only question about it is—shall I find anything worth recording in this quiet, country existence? Well, it pleases me to begin with such a trifle as my own enjoyment in this property I have bought, and, after all, I am writing for myself and not for others.

My ability to retire and settle down at the early age of forty is a cause of gratitude to the Gods of Chance, who gave me such rapid commercial success in the 'slump' years when so many others were feeling the pinch. I just happened to strike the right propositions all the time, and now I can play the Squire in my new "domain" and look forward to the idyllic life which next summer will bring, fishing and pottering about these beautiful, unspoilt backwaters. Not that I despise the country and its pursuits in winter—being country-bred—particularly in this fine old house. I shall find all the entertainment I need for the long evenings sorting through the books and all the lumber with which it is stocked, and by next winter I hope to have made friends who will come round for billiards or cards.

Perhaps I may marry again, for 'Heronay' should possess a hostess, but I fear I could never bring to another union the zeal of my first romantic attachment, so quickly ended in one of the London air raids.

I feel myself lucky to have got 'Heronay' at such a bargain price, and suppose it would have cost me a good few thousands more, but for the bad name it derives from its former occupant. After standing empty, however, for so many years, the dilapidation was great, and I could see how the agents jumped at my offer.

It is rather strange how a house can continue bear an ill repute from the misdemeanours of a tenant, even years alter his or her death, though no doubt this place holds very gruesome associations for many of the local residents. One can excuse Harper his crimes on the ground of his undeniable lunacy, but his 'reign of terror', conducted from here, must have been a ghastly period for the neighbourhood, especially in view of the shocking mutilations he always practised. Still, he died long ago in Broadmoor, and it is thought that the ground was cleared of all his victims. I have had the exterior entirely re-faced, and I think 'Heronay' may now claim to be purged of his influence.

Well, I seem to be rambling on—a good start for the diary, any-way, if I can keep it up! Now I will close for today, and spend the rest of the evening looking over my new possessions.

November 18th.

A bright day for the time of year, crisp and frosty. Had a call from the vicar, who asked, among other things, if I proposed to join the local Hunt. Told him that I was no horseman, but hoped to do a bit of shooting when more completely settled. He then touched on the poor maniac, my predecessor, and I asked him if he thought the dreadful record of the place would affect my welcome in the village. He replied that he was sure the people in the other big houses would soon forget Harper when they realised the hospitality of the new owner and saw how the whole estate had been cleansed of its former unkempt appearance. The villagers, though, would take longer to accept me to their confidence, and I must not be surprised if tradesmen refused to deliver goods after dark, as the grounds of 'Heronay' were popularly supposed to be haunted. He made his exit, after inviting me to dinner next week, when he promised I should meet some of my new neigh-bours at the vicarage. I shall welcome the change from solitude, alt-hough my evenings here will not be dull while I have so many of Harper's belongings to look through. He appears to have had no next -of-kin, which accounts for all the furniture being sold with the house. Before his dementia overtook him he must have been a man of refinement. His library is a book-lover's paradise, and his personal knick-knacks and ornaments mostly of quite intrinsic value. While rummaging in the drawers of the study desk last night I found a remarkably fine meerschaum pipe, which he must have smoked for many years, to judge by the degree of coloration of the bowl. It has an amber mouthpiece set in gold and is, in fact, quite an ornament. I intend to clean it up and give it a place of honour on the mantel-shelf. My man can polish it when he starts on the china. As an ex-army batman, polishing is a hobby with him. Incidentally, I must consider engaging a staff of servants now that I am about to meet new people. Jobson can manage quite well in a flat, as he has done for so long during my City career, but we shall need more than occasional daily help if we are to entertain as I hope to be entertained. That's all for today. I shall consult the local registry—if any—in the morning.

November 19th.

An irritating set-back today. Called on Miss Simms the post-mistress, who acts as domestic registrar, and she promised to send round some applicants for my household jobs. Left her, thinking the matter as good as settled, and stayed at home till lunch-time, but nobody called. Now she has rung up to say that she 'can find no one suitable at the moment'. On reflection, I thought her a bit evasive during the interview, and am inclined to suspect the cause is all this superstitious rubbish the vicar mentioned. Suppose I shall have to get servants from elsewhere, but it is very ridiculous. My alterations have given the place quite a modern appearance, and there is nothing sinister about the grounds at night. Evidently the local proletariat keep dwelling on the secret burials that used to take place, and imagination has done the rest.

Spent the earlier part of the evening thinking things over, and planning for the future. I must seriously consider taking another wife. She might solve the servant problem more readily, and a hostess is really essential for entertaining married guests; but I don't fancy the notion a bit. Mary's memory is still too fresh even after all these years... Perhaps a lady housekeeper?

Jobson has made ;a splendid job of the meerschaum, which looks, as I said before, definitely ornamental. I have a great fancy for this class of pipe myself, though I have never achieved such superb 'colour' in any of my own. I am, in fact, tempted to sterilise the stem of this one and see how it tastes. It should prove a ripe smoke. It has never occurred to me before to smoke another man's pipe—much less that of a homicidal maniac—but I think washing the mouthpiece with Lysol and scouring the bowl stem with a hot wire should destroy any possible germs...

November 20th.

I carried out my intention before retiring last night, and so enjoyed my smoke that I felt disinclined for writing up any more of this diary. With a load of my favourite tobacco, and a good fire in the study, the time passed like lightning. Really speaking, I think I must have dozed, though the meerschaum was still burning well when I saw by the clock that it was well past my usual bedtime. Today I feel rather unrested, though I was sleeping soundly when Jobson called me.

Most likely I have spent too much time indoors lately browsing among the relics of Harper's tenancy. When I am getting daily fresh air and exercise I never dream—but I am under the impression that my sleep was disturbed last night, though I cannot recall any details. I shall take a walk round the grounds now and blow the cobwebs away before lunch...

Later:

My morning walk very beneficial and brightened by parading my new acquisition. Saw the Vicar and Dr. Corbett, the local G.P, passing my drive gates, and they complimented me on the 'colour' of it. As they made no reference to Harper I took it they did not recognise it as his, and I did not choose to enlighten them. My ramble took me to a strip of waste ground enclosed by a shrubbery and a walk where, I am told, two of Harper's victims were buried—their trunks at least. It seemed an ideal spot for a murder, and I could almost enter into his distorted point of view—at least as far as the spice of secrecy was concerned.

There must be a grim fascination in committing a crime that rouses the countryside and then watching the police go off on false scents. Harper went about his butchery for months without attracting the least suspicion. Evidently he can have shown no outward symptom of insanity between the attacks, and must have exercised amazing caution in executing his horrible tasks; yet his dementia was of an extreme kind, as was shown by the distorted artistry of his mutilations.

Employed the afternoon and evening in a fruitless journey to the County town—twenty miles away—in search of domestics. Interviewed several candidates who happened to be at the Registry Office, but as soon as I mentioned my address they made various excuses not to accept service with me. The popular aversion to 'Heronay' is very widespread, it seems, and it looks as if I shall have to engage my staff in London. Most annoying.

Found some newspaper cuttings in the course of my evening's exploring among Harper's belongings. They all related to his criminal career, and I could picture him gloating over the horror which his monstrous 'recreation' was instilling in the public mind. Having been abroad at the time I was not "well up" in the history of this butcher, and so took the trouble to read the cuttings through. Apparently he was actuated by no personal motives but from a general lust to kill, and his victims were invariably women. The most revolting feature of the murders was his habit of severing the head and limbs with a sharp hatchet and leaving them on the scene for identification, while carrying away the trunk for addition to a sort of 'musaeum' which is supposed to have been kept in some room of the house.

The subsequent interring seems only to have been effected when decomposition rendered it necessary, as the police deduced from the remains.

November 21st.

Another disturbed night, judging by this morning's lassitude—though again I have no clear recollection of my dreams beyond the feeling that they were of a distressing and even frightening nature. Also I am convinced that I did—for me—quite an unprecedented thing. I noticed earth stains on my feet when getting into my bath, and Jobson found more of them on the bed-linen, from which it is clear that I must have walked in my sleep. I have always regarded this as a sign of mental unbalance, so told Jobson I had gone down to the garden, fancying I heard an intruder. He must have wondered why I did not wear my slippers, but is too well trained to offer such criticism. I have never had a day's illness in my life, and I do not like this symptom of nerve trouble—especially as I spent most of yester-day out-of-doors. I shall spend today on the links and get my lunch at the Club House.

Later:

A splendid game of golf with a member to whom the Secretary introduced me, and another round, by myself, in the afternoon. I should sleep well tonight. Meanwhile, a sensation has arisen in the village by the discovery of a dead body in Arningham Woods. It appears to be a case of murder, the victim being a young girl from a gypsy encampment nearby. The postman told me that her throat had been cut and that one of the hands, severed at the wrist, was missing.

The last I take to be a piece of village gossip originating in Harper's dismembering proclivities. I understand the affair is regarded as probably a crime of jealousy and that the police are looking for a young basket maker who left the camp this morning.

Enough diary for today. Just half an hour's smoke, and I shall not want any rocking.

November 22nd.

Once more a shockingly restless night—this time caused by definite nightmares. Though I fell asleep at once and do not remem-ber awakening until Jobson brought my tea, I feel as if I had been 'on the tiles'. Most of the time I seemed to be pacing endless corridors and clambering up and down stairs burdened by some weighty object which I was trying to conceal. What it was I cannot remember, except that it seemed both precious and repulsive simultaneously, and that I was in a panic in case anyone should find me with it. I examined my feet on rising for any traces of sleep-walking, but could find no such evidence. One thing, however, puzzled me—namely, that I appeared to be wearing different pyjamas from those in which I went to bed. Still, most of my sleeping-suits resemble each other, being all black silk and varying only in the braiding, so I may have been mistaken. Somnambulism apart, though, if these exhausting dreams continue I must ask Corbett for a tonic. It will be a good opportunity to mention the matter if I can persuade him to a round of golf this afternoon.

Later:

I was wrong, it would seem, to start this diary wondering if I should find enough to write about in so rural a spot. The murder of the gypsy girl has now been followed by the mysterious disappearance of a cottager's daughter. By a coincidence she is one of the prospective aids I interviewed two days ago, and, although in service in the County Town, was spending the week-end here with her family.

Apparently she went out for a solitary walk late last evening and she has not been seen since, nor has she returned to her employer's residence. The discovery of blood-stains in a little-used lane near the village has, of course, given rise to a crop of ugly rumours, but as none of the girl's clothing or belongings has come to light I see no reason to connect the two facts. Quite probably a case of elopement...

I was about to close my diary for the day when Jobson entered my study in a great state of agitation. He had been taking a moonlight walk in the grounds near one of the boundary walls when he noticed some unusual object in a tussock of grass. Stooping to examine it, he saw, to his horror, that it was a human hand! As he finished describing the finding of it he produced the horrible thing from a roll of newspaper and laid it on my desk, when, overcoming my natural revulsion, I inspected it under a powerful reading-lamp. Though no student of anatomy, I judged it to be the hand of a woman, partly, I dare say, on account of the cheap and gaudy rings which adorned two of the fingers. These baubles seemed, in a vague way, familiar, and I supposed that I had seen their wearer at some time in the village. Naturally, I rang up the police without loss of time, and have spent the last hour talking with the Inspector—a very capable man who, as a young member of the Force, was instrumental in Harper's arrest. He not only confirmed the rumour of the gypsy's hand having been cut off, but positively identified it with Jobson's grim "find". He thinks that the basket-maker, an unsuccessful suitor, must have taken the hand as a keepsake and then, fearing to keep so terrible a reminder, have thrown it over my wall in his flight. This theory gives them a clue to the direction in which he was travelling, and the inspector spoke hopefully of an early arrest.

November 26th.

The events of the past few days have occupied my mind to the exclusion of all other matters. My diary has been neglected, and I must recapitulate. So far from rustic uneventfulness, I seem to have landed myself in the middle of a Grand Guignol play.

A fresh series of crimes identical with those of my perverted predecessor has broken out in the neighbourhood, and the surrounding country is teeming with police, press men, and morbid sightseers. By having the gates locked I have been able to keep most of them off this property, but I caught two reporters astride the wall near Harper's "cemetery" yesterday, and had Jobson turn them away. The village is in a state of siege, as no woman will venture out after dark, and even by daylight they go in twos and threes. A rumour that Harper had not died at Broadmoor, but had escaped, rapidly gained ground, and I found myself wondering if this were the case. The police, however, assure me that he died years ago and that, so far from any such escape being 'hushed up', a warning would be broadcast to all districts. Hard upon the heels of Jobson's discovery of the hand came news of a second mutilation during the ensuing night. The head, arms, and legs of Dr. Corbett's cook were found lying on a tombstone in the churchyard. The torso was missing. The night after, another woman's head and limbs were left neatly piled by the roadside not far from the Assembly Rooms. They must have been placed there in the early morning hours, as a local dance held there was not over till well after midnight. It is very disturbing to have this dangerous lunatic on one's doorstep, apart from the noisy crowd of sightseers who came to pry around—and even picnic on!—the sites of his crimes. To add to all this discord (and perhaps resulting from it) my own health is causing me serious anxiety. It seems impossible for me to get a decent night's rest even with the sedative that Corbett prescribed. My sleep is constantly broken by the most hideous nightmares, in one of which, last night, I even dreamt that I was accompanying Harper on one of his nocturnal escapades. The beginning of the dream remains utterly chaotic, but I distinctly remember standing in a field over the corpse of a woman whom he had dismembered.

Though I could not see the man distinctly he seemed to be constantly at my side compelling me to busy myself hiding the traces of his handiwork. As often, I believe, happens in dreams when we do things as a matter of course that are completely foreign to our natures, I felt myself lacking all volition to resist Harper's influence and, in fact, quite entering into the spirit of his requirements. I buried the woman's clothes in a ditch, covering them carefully with earth and dead bracken, and arranged parts of the body on a gate, balancing the head on one post and hanging the limbs in a row on the bars. The rest of the nightmare is like a fogged photographic plate, save that I repeated my former impression of tramping great distances with a heavy burden—in this instance a nude female torso.

Such ghastly dreams must indicate some kind of ill-health, and if Corbett cannot stop them I shall consult a specialist.

Later:

Jobson has just come back from the village with fresh news which, to me at any rate, appears horribly significant. Another woman's head and limbs have been found, balanced on a gate dividing two nearby pastures. Jobson's description corresponds unpleasantly with my dream. Is it possible that I am somehow spiritually *en rapport* with Harper's ghost through the medium of a common dwelling-place? I have never imagined myself in the least 'psychic'. And then, how explain the finding of an actual corpse (or, at any rate, parts of one) in view of Harper's decease? No: obviously a different maniac, but with similar tendencies, must be at large, and I do not see why the 'aura' of Harper's possessions should bring me in touch with *him*— unless, perhaps, there is some malignant 'elemental' native to these parts which prompts the killings and which may, to some extent, influence anybody living locally. But this is too wild a speculation. I have never believed in such things. Jobson, by the way, found a telegram for him at the Post-Office telling him of a sister's illness. He is a sterling friend and servant, so I told him that he must, of course, take a few days off to see her. He demurred at first on the ground that I should be unable to get local help, but I could see he really wanted to go. He has accordingly left to catch a late train, and I have the house to myself.

November 27th.

Another outrage last night, and another nightmare for me! This time it is Miss Simms, the post-mistress, whose remains were found on her own counter by her daily help, who arrives to make early tea at seven o'clock. The unfortunate woman can have had no chance to resist her attacker as, though she had neighbours on both sides, no outcry was heard. The trunk, as usual, had been carried off. Whether my nightmare had, again, any connection with this crime I cannot recall. I am only aware of the sensation, to which I have now grown accustomed, of carrying things about and of being a fugitive. Towards morning however, I had an amazingly vivid dream to the effect that I came down the stairs from an upper floor at present disused, entered the bathroom and carefully washed my hands and feet, without, for some reason, turning on the light. This recollection came back as soon as I opened my eyes, and, being convinced that I had been guilty of actual sleep-walking on at least one previous occasion, I went at once to the bathroom to look for traces of my suspected earlier visit. But nothing turned out to be disarranged, and I was left in doubt until, after preparing and eating a light breakfast, I decided to explore the upstairs rooms.

One of the first things to catch my eye was a black tassel, similar to those of my pyjama girdles, projecting from under a locked door. I remembered having seen the key to this door hanging in a cupboard under the main staircase, but on going to get it found it had disap-peared, and I am now forced to a conclusion that I hate to face. Apart from the evidence of somnambulism, which, in itself, I resent as a weakness, I cannot overlook the connection between my dreams and the nightly butchery that is being enacted.

Is it conceivable that, in my sleeping state, I have been actually present at one or more of these murders, and even—dreadful thought! —handled the dismembered cadavers? My whole mind shrinks from this theory; but it is otherwise hard to explain the subconscious urge to wash, the locking up of a (possibly *stained*) pyjama suit, and the hiding of the keys. Good God! I must be under hypnotic suggestion, and if I am seen and recognised in this state I shall be thought guilty of the actual crimes themselves!

It has occurred to me that my bad nights may be due to excessive smoking—for I have lately been inseparable from my—or rather Harper's—meerschaum. To test this I shall abstain from it tonight and make do with a couple of cigarettes.

November 28th.

It is finished. And the meerschaum pipe is burnt in the largest fire I could build into my grate! I only write this last page of my diary for the sake of my next-of-kin—to assure them that, whatever my own condition, there is no *hereditary* taint. The pipe alone was to blame. When my writing is done I shall go out into the grounds and shoot myself under God's clean daylit sky!

I stuck to my intention of smoking nothing stronger than cigarettes, and for the first time in a week passed the early hours of the night in untroubled repose. Later, however, the restlessness must have returned, for a falling log awoke me to find myself sitting by the study fire—smoking the meerschaum. As I came to full consciousness I experienced the sudden waning of an abstract horror—indefinable but intense. It passed so quickly, though, that within a few seconds I doubted its very existence. Everything seemed normal, the room was still comfortably warm, and I felt too wide awake to seek my bed at once. Instead I said aloud and quite cheerfully, 'Well, if my sleep-walking only brings me down here for a smoke, there's no great harm done,' and as the meerschaum was drawing satisfactorily I decided to sit up and finish it. If only I had suspected and burned the damnable thing then! An habitual smoker always derives a soothing effect from puffing at a pipe, and it was the marked superiority of the meerschaum in this respect that had attached me to it so strongly. Now, within a few moments, so pleasant a drowsiness crept over me that I heaped more logs on the fire, determined to finish the night where I sat rather than risk finally arousing myself by a journey back to bed. But if sleep came back—and it did, heavily—it was not the revitalising, dreamless slumber that I wanted, hut a fantastic string of the disjointed nightmare scenes in which I was constantly hunted from place to place by unseen pursuers and carrying in my arms a naked torso. At length these visions gave way to a sort of silent, oppressive darkness, and that, in turn, to pictures of my own earlier life: so that I shook off the menace of the former and looked happily at sane and wholesome things.

I forgot that Mary had long been dead, and thought that she lay beside me in our old room at Hampstead. She was asleep, to judge by her quietness, and I had just awakened; but she lay very still in my arms. I bent my head forward and tried to touch her face with my lips—but it eluded me—and, with an effort, I opened my eyes. I was back in my own bed at 'Heronay', and, of course, there was no face on the pillow beside me.

Yet I did indeed hold something in my arms down under the bedclothes—something that felt like the body of a woman, *but was very cold and still.* I slid my feet out of the floor *sideways without turning back the sheet.*

The missing bunch of keys lay on my pedestal cupboard, but I shall not belatedly explore that upper room. I know too well what it contains.

HAUNTED AIR

'WELL, BLAKE, we can't do your stuff yet. What about another "tonic" while we wait?'

Pitchmann, air-record breaker and taxi-pilot of international repute, pushed his empty tankard over the counter and strolled to the window, where he stood looking glumly through rain-blurred glass across the sodden aerodrome.

Violent gusts howled in paroxysms about the angles of the Club House, and the wind-stocking above the hangars stood out horizontally, threshing like a mad thing.

'Okay,' said the press photographer laconically. 'My squeak, I think. Two more cans, please, steward.'

Pitchmann moved back to the bar.

'Bloody nuisance hanging about this god-forsaken dive for a shot of that blasted crash,' he complained. 'Why the hell didn't Carr pick some tin-pot shopkeeper for a passenger instead of an M.P? Your rag would have given 'em a three-line par and let me out of this "picnic".'

Blake shrugged and took a pull at his beer. He knew Pitchmann as well as anyone could claim to know him, having been his passenger on many rush jobs across Europe, and he knew when the big pilot expected an answer—which was not often.

Pitchmann half emptied his tankard at a gulp and swept the four other occupants of the room with a contemptuous glance, favouring the Club Instructor with a nod as nearly cordial as the latter might care to believe.

'Better join us, Jacobs,' he remarked acidly, with an imperious gesture to the barman. 'You seem to think it's too breezy for your nestful of stiffs to take the air—so why waste good beer-time?'

Jacobs hitched his chair forward and murmured, 'Thanks. A pink gin,' endeavouring to sound as casual as he could. He hated Pitchmann's intolerant grey eyes and air of conscious superiority, but knew that his directors expected tact from him—perhaps even more than flying ability. He was not obliged to agree with all Pitchmann's opinions, but it would not do to offend the fellow.

'Shot if I'm going up solo in this gale, anyway,' said young Remington, who, as an owner-pilot with private means, held aces in no particular esteem.

Pitchmann pointedly ignored him, rousing the boy to quick anger.

'Call it what you like,' he went on heatedly, 'it was taking a chance yesterday in this sort of damned weather that killed Carr, threw his passenger clean out of the machine, and brought you vultures up here to get photos of his wreckage.' His second remark drew the badger. Pitchmann accorded him a supercilious stare.

'That poor mutt!' he replied witheringly. 'He was for the high jump all his flying career. Windy as hell. Fair weather pilot from A to Z. That's the only way he lasted so long. I've seen him turn down local joy-rides on account of a bit of ground mist when Imperials were getting through from Le Bourget in pea-soup stuff. You blokes who play at flying for a hobby can go up and sun yourselves on fine days like damned butterflies, but the professional has to fly in anything—anything,' he repeated loudly, 'otherwise aviation ceases to be a business.' He turned his back on Remington and glanced at Jacobs for confirmation. The latter nodded judicially.

'That's true up to a point,' he agreed, 'but we all have our different jobs. Mine's training pupils at present, and I'm not expected to risk their necks and the machines in these conditions.' He glanced out of the window and added, 'Incidentally, the sun is breaking through a bit, though the wind's increasing!'

'Come on, Blake,' said Pitchmann, slamming down his tankard. 'It's visibility we want. Damn the wind! Let's get your plates exposed, and we can be back in Town by evening!'

He stooped to pick up his gloves and turned impatiently to the press photographer, who was finishing his drink. 'Get a jerk on, man. I want to be away.'

The door slammed after them.

'He's rather wonderful, don't you think?' observed the only lady member present, looking up from the pages of *Air Events*, and emerging from daydreams of a celebrated woman pilot's latest exploit. 'I mean,' she continued diffidently as nobody vouchsafed a reply, 'a man has to be big really big in himself—to talk quite so—so ruthlessly, to—to lay down the law like Captain Pitchmann.'

'Damn good pilot, anyway,' said Jacobs, breaking an awkward silence. The barman was heard to grunt noncommittally. Young Remington lit a cigarette and blew a smoke ring ceilingwards.

'You may think he's wonderful, Mrs. Conyer,' he volunteered, 'I think he's a disease. After all, *"De Mortuis nil nisi bonum."* I didn't know Carr personally, but that was no way to talk of a bloke who's just passed out...'

The roar of an engine drowned the rest of his sentence and Pitchmann's 'plane flashed past one of the windows, staggering drunkenly in the tremendous gusts that assailed it. As the noise dwindled the fourth occupant of the lounge broke in for the first time.

'Thanks, laddie. I *did* know Carr personally. We were, in fact, very old friends. But it's no good arguing with a man like Pitchmann. A good pilot, yes—very good—but absolutely without sentiment, so one can't expect any consideration from him.' He paused and stared after the disappearing aircraft.

'Pitchmann,' he resumed thoughtfully, 'accused Carr of being "windy", and implied that it was a lack of *technique* in bad conditions that killed him. I *know* how he was killed, and, if you like, I will tell you at the risk of straining your credulity... Do any of you believe in ghosts?' he wound up with apparent irrelevance.

'Suggesting a supernatural explanation of the crash?' Jacobs countered. 'Because, if so, Beckett, you're wrong. Carr was caught in a bad "bump"—a "sinker"—and thrown out of control. I know the air pockets there, and they're fierce enough even in a normal breeze.

'Haven't you seen that Air Ministry notice advising pilots not to cross the Ridgeway in a high wind under two thousand feet? They have quite a few spots black-listed that way now—one near "Gib", for instance—another up the Forth. Queer things, bumps.'

'First of all,' said Beckett, settling back with the persistence of a born raconteur and totally disregarding Jacobs' remark, 'I must say in fairness to Carr that he was not a fair-weather pilot. When I was his observer in France, in 1916, we were up more than a few times in this sort of thing'—he waved a hand towards the window—'and in a type of machine that would fall to bits on you for two pins. Carr never flunked his job then, but as he explained to me when I met him years later in civil flying, he didn't see the force of taking unreasonable risks in peace time for the sake of publicity. He preferred knocking up a modest three or four hundred a year in his own way to undertaking spectacular flights for big money which he might not live to enjoy. Hence his reputation as quoted by Pitchmann and his failure to get work with the more progressive concerns. He and Pitchmann often used to meet at Croydon, and the great man never missed a chance of using Carr as a foil for his own prowess. He would watch Carr take a passenger to a thousand feet for a couple of loops, and then go up and cut the air all shapes, at a quarter the height. Carr could have done it as well, and *had* done later in the War, when he was on "scouts", but people didn't know that, and his caution lost him a lot of trade, not that he seemed to care. I guess his wife knocked the personal ambition out of him—but that's by the way.

'Now, I'm going to tell you something about Carr that I'll bet he never admitted to a soul except myself; but first I must digress to explain what helped me to believe his story. You look interested, Mrs. Conyer, and if you two blokes don't want to listen, you can play darts. We shan't fly yet, anyway.

'Well, I had a brother who was a pilot in the East, after the War, operating from a hill station—frontier stuff you know—and he was killed in much the same way as poor old Carr. One night, after the rains, a pretty extensive landslide occurred in his district, a few thousand tons of soil falling on a native settlement, and my brother was sent up to survey the damage. When he failed to return after a due interval, two machines went to look for him. Of these, only one returned, the pilot reporting that his companion had first sighted my brother's plane, badly smashed up among some rocks, and had dived down ostensibly for a closer investigation. Seeing that there was no possible landing-place at hand, the reporting pilot had kept his altitude and circled round waiting for the other to climb up again when his survey had finished. To his astonishment the machine below suddenly began to perform the most crazy aerobatics, throwing several loops and rolls at a very low altitude and finally flying for some distance on its back, from which position it presently nose-dived with great violence into the rocks, and burst into flames. After debating for some time the advisability of investigating both crashes more closely, he concluded that they might have been caused by abnormal wind eddies, and that it would be wiser to send a land party. This the C.O. decided to do, and after considerable difficulty the crashes were brought in, and the usual court enquiry held. Both pilots had evidently been killed instantly, but from my brother's machine, which had not fired, it was deduced that there had been no structural failure, and the verdict was "Crashed out of control, owing to exceptional atmospheric phenomena associated with the contours". Within a few weeks three more pilots were killed at or near the same spot, after which it was mapped out as a prohibited area, and the matter officially closed. It was only when I met an officer from the same squadron on leave during the following year that I heard about the native version as related by a fanatical old tribesman, who had made a pilgrimage to the aerodrome especially to implore the C.O. to stop flying over the landslide, and had talked a lot of guff about *"Things which are Enemies of Man and Beast Creation"* and the Earth having *"Given Outlet to That which the Prophet had Sealed Down"*. Guff, we called it then,' said Beckett quietly. 'I'm not so sure now.'

It was a tribute to the man's personality and to the conviction in his voice that no word of interruption was spoken as he slowly filled his pipe.

'As you, no doubt, are aware,' he went on presently, 'there was a landslide on this saddle called the Ridgeway some ten days ago, but what you may not know is that Carr was the first pilot to fly over it after the occurrence. He read the account of it in a newspaper, and, having his joy-ride 'plane parked in a field relatively near to the scene, he elected to go up and view the subsidence from the air. It is of interest that his machine was an Avro three-seater, convertible for dual control by removing the middle seat, flooring and all, so as to expose the second rudder-bar and joystick socket. Carr had been giving instruction to some local resident the previous evening, and he took the Avro over the Ridgeway, flying from the front seat, without bothering to remove the dual controls. Well, he found the place without difficulty—a big brown gash in the green hillside, as he described it, but nothing much as a spectacle. Beyond blocking a short length of road in the valley, the fallen earth seemed to have done little harm, and he was about to turn. back to his field when he caught sight of something moving in the air, between his 'plane and the ground, which looked extremely odd, and, as he told me, gave him an unaccountable feeling of goose flesh, even before he saw what sort of thing it was.

'Apart from its extraordinary shade of pulsating, unnatural green, the object was quite evidently not a bird, and he might momentarily have dubbed it a grotesque toy balloon, like the flying pigs they shoot down at the Hendon Pageant, but for the fact that it was so obviously—and somehow *horribly*—alive. Carr described it as resembling a monstrous monkey, clambering with incredible speed up an invisible rope. It appeared to be *wriggling* vertically upwards, and as he watched it in fascinated wonder his lower wing passed over and hid it from view. He banked steeply to the left, failed to see it, and as quickly whipped into a right-hand turn—but the green thing had vanished. He made a complete circle, still without success, and finally, the air being calm, took his hands from the controls and half raised himself in his seat, the better to see over the engine cowling. As he did so, the machine's nose rose abruptly, and he had to grab the joystick in a hurry to avoid a stall.

'Carr told me that he was too intent on watching for the reappearance of the weird object to realise at once how queerly the aeroplane had behaved. It was so rigged that, without ballast in the rear cockpit, the nose should have dropped. As soon as this dawned on him, he again released the stick, which, to his utter amazement, began to move rapidly from side to side, the Avro wallowing in unison with it, as the ailerons took effect. So pronounced and regular was the movement that it could only be caused by someone moving the dual stick in the other cockpit—but he had taken off *solo*!

'Carr said that several things happened to his brain during the next few seconds, but in what order he could not remember. Ill-defined fear numbed his faculties, so that he could do nothing but stare stupidly at the shifting controls, but at the same time a corner of his mind, working with crystal clarity, was aware that the green thing had somehow got into the machine with him, that it was definitely alive, though equally definitely not human, and, worst of all, that it was *intelligently* operating stick and rudder! He felt his hair crawling under his tightly strapped helmet, and dared not look behind him.

'Presently he heard the engine open out, and dully realised that the throttle lever was correspondingly moving forward while, at the same time, the joystick came back slowly towards him, and the Avro began to climb. He seems at this period to have fallen into a sort of coma, in which state his physical senses were blanked out, and only some deep recess of his brain continued to record intuitive impressions. He knew that, whatever creature was riding behind him, it was age-old, and somehow *belonged* to the air. He also knew that it had been long imprisoned, and was exultant at release, while he understood, too, that there was no novelty in this nightmare situation.

'Either it had happened before, or, his subconscious self had contained a fore-knowledge of it, hitherto mercifully concealed... His next physical impression was seeing the needle of the altimeter standing at five thousand feet, and simultaneously feeling the 'plane nose down into a power dive, engine at full throttle, and stick pressing the dashboard. For a few seconds it held this course, then swept up and over in a perfect loop. As the stick came back into the pit of his stomach he clutched it feebly—childishly—and attempted to force it away, but it was locked as though in a vice. While the sunlit vista of Earth whirled over his head, the stick did go forward again, but Carr knew *he* had not moved it. An instant later, the Avro executed a flick roll, stalled, and fell into a spin.

'Carr said that as fast as the thought flashed into his brain, that this was the end, it was followed by a positive assurance that his strange captor would let him live—at least for a time. He felt, in some fashion, that this same horror had befallen other pilots whose deaths had never been satisfactorily accounted for, and that, becoming demented with fear, they had roused contemptuous anger in these green things, and so courted instant death. He, by showing no physical reaction, had whetted the appetite of this monstrosity for a cat-and-mouse game. He said he felt like a raw pupil receiving a lesson in aerobatics from a masterly instructor.

'Carr said the culmination of nausea was reached when the thing touched him for the first time (I gather it forced other assignations on him, though of these he did not speak). Powerless to make physical resistance, he felt a pad-like extremity brush his cheek clammily, and expected a stranglehold, but realised with extreme repugnance, that the touch was in the nature of a petting. The viscous paw passed smoothly over his face, covering his eyes, where it lingered caressingly, obscuring his vision. Then, to his profound disgust, he felt a gelatinous mouth pressed against his own! The shudder that passed through him at the contact somehow restored his muscular control, and, uttering a word of loathing, he again clutched the controls, dimly aware that the green thing was crawling sinuously over the side to the port lower plane, where it wreathed itself about the gap strut and stood regarding him. Carr described it as resembling a human or ape in build, having a flexible trunk, four limbs ending in flat, webbed pads, and a grotesquely tiny wet head, with round, mouse-like ears. Its mouth was a yellow slit, and its eyes lidless, and opaque. It was nude and hairless, but of indeterminate sex, as it possessed the faculty of altering its shape in any direction, like those glutinous, transparent things one finds in ponds. When he at last brought himself to look directly at it, the creature grinned at him, and hopped along the wing, where it gripped an aileron and shook it up and down, causing the machine to rock. Next, it stretched two of its rubber-like limbs the full length of the fuselage, to seize rudder and elevators, which it proceeded to operate by direct pressure against Carr's efforts with the controls. From this unique position it once more put the plane through all its imaginable paces. During the whole performance its face radiated a sort of perverse glee, reminding Carr, through the mist of horror that wrapped him, of a mischievous child playing with a toy. Finally it slithered back along the wing, and gazed intently and for a long time into Carr's face. Carr said that its telepathic influence was strongest at that time. He knew as well as if it had spoken aloud what it was thinking. There was a damnable, triumphant possessiveness in its eyes which told him that he now belonged to the green thing for all Eternity. It recalled, he said, the way some women look at a man when they have him in their power. I suppose he spoke from experience. Finally the creature released its hold, and drifted down into the abyss of air, still staring up at him with an expression of gloating ownership.

'Carr said he must have found his way back to his field, and landed there quite automatically. His next conscious recollection was of leaning against a tree sobbing like a baby, while an alarmed mechanic offered him a cup of water.'

Beckett came to an abrupt halt, but, seeing that the others were waiting for him to continue, added briefly: 'That was all Carr told me.

I never saw him alive again.'

'My God!' whispered Mrs. Conyer. 'What a ghastly idea!' She stopped, looked helplessly at the others, and went on, 'Forgive me, Mr. Beckett, but did—did your friend drink?'

Beckett shook his head.

'No more than I do or any of us here. Personally, I believe Carr's account. You must please yourselves what construction you put on it.'

He relapsed into thoughtful silence.

'Why in God's name did he go back to the Ridgeway yesterday?' asked young Remington, obviously deeply impressed.

Beckett shrugged.

'Nobody could guess the active range of such a—manifestation,' he replied. 'Carr's flight started in the opposite direction, and maybe the green thing found him and took him there. The passenger fell out, you know, nearly two miles away, and *that* hasn't been explained. I think he *jumped!*'

Jacobs had been staring moodily at the carpet during the whole of Beckett's recital. Now he straightened up, and gave him a very curious glance.

'Sorry,' he began, 'but this is right outside my experience or understanding. I see you're sincere, Beckett, and I won't be such a swine as to laugh, especially after Pitchmann's behaviour. But no! Sorry, I can't—!'

The harsh 'burr' of the telephone interrupted him. The barman picked up the receiver, and they heard him answering the call.

'Yes. Speaking. What's that? Whereabouts? Good Lord! Both of them? What's that? A mile?'

He turned from the instrument to Jacobs. 'Ridge Village Police, sir,' he announced. 'Captain Pitchmann's crashed.'

Mrs. Conyer and Remington sprang spontaneously to their feet.

'Where?' Jacobs demanded.

'On the Ridgeway sir, close to Mr. Carr's Avro.'

'Are they—all right?' Jacobs managed with an effort. The barman shook his head gravely.

'No. Both killed. The Sergeant thinks the gale got them out of control. Mr. Blake was flung out a mile away.'

Beckett crossed his legs, and knocked out his pipe on his boot-heel.

'As you remarked just now, Jacobs,' he put in quietly. 'Queer things—Bumps.'

THE IRON SWINE

I DON'T KNOW just why it is that Beckett—the fellow who told us about the green ghosts of the air the day Pitchmann was killed—is always the nucleus of any debate in our little flying club when talk veers towards the supernatural. In any case, it's a bit unusual to find the membership of such an institution taking the subject seriously. Most flying people are materialists, more or less, and apparently unimaginative, but Beckett is evidently keen on spooks, and, being a war-time pilot with plenty of seniority, doesn't hesitate to take a chance on ridicule about his pet subject. He's pretty hard boiled, and so receives little open contradiction from the most sceptical, whilst the majority of us find him well worth listening to, whatever our private views.

The local vicar, an admirably broad-minded man, who was a Flying Corps *padre* in the year dot, often drops in for a drink and a chat, and it was on the occasion of one of his visits that the conversation turned upon the nautical superstition that ships have souls. The vicar was, perhaps surprisingly, a protagonist of this belief, and maintained that it was in no way at variance with the tenets of his Faith. He argued, I recall, that some part of the personalities of designer and workman might easily be imparted to a vessel under construction, though nobody present seemed able to produce any convincing evidence.

It was here that Beckett chimed in, with his usual air of calm assurance, and supported the vicar with the affirmation that he knew at least one aeroplane possessed of a soul—and a damned malicious one, at that.

129

'It is one of those foreign, all-metal jobs,' he began, 'built of ribbed duralumin, of course, for lightness, but it looked like a sheet of corrugated iron, flying around with a hunch-backed whale-like body stuck amidships. I flew the beastly thing a bit at one time, and my term of endearment for it was "The Iron Swine". As far as I know, the designer only built one of them, and then went broke, because he couldn't get the type taken up for production. By tile time he finished the yarn those of you who follow aviation history will know the kite I'm talking about—but "no names, no pack-drill".

'Handling the brute, even in fair weather, was like pushing a lump of pig-iron around the sky, and on a rough day it was an abortion. The most severely practical blokes who flew it hated the thing, and I personally sensed its sullen antagonism first time I had it aloft. On full engine it would sometimes fly quite well so far as normal banking turns went, but as soon as you throttled down for an approach, it began to buck. It had no gliding angle, as one understands the term on reasonable aircraft. Either it would stick its hog nose down and dive at the deck like a falling house, or, if you held it back anywhere near stalling speed, it began to flick and twitch against your control for all the world like a freshly caught fish. The only way to make sure of landing properly was to "rumble" in with a spot of engine, and, even then, it would either try to overshoot the aerodrome or drop out of your hands in a fast "pancake".

'Well, that animated lump of metal is still on the list of registered aircraft, and it has belonged, to my knowledge, to at least five different private owners. It has killed all but one of them. The amazing thing is that it has done its killing without ever being seriously crashed. My belief is that it's too blasted crafty. It hates pilots, but it doesn't want to die itself!

'Its first victim was a laddie with more money than brains, who bought it to show off to his friends. It's a big beast, and will carry ten passengers comfortably.

'To avoid any chance of action for slander on the part of the designer—a man I should be psychologically interested to meet—I'll name the owners fictitiously but alphabetically, calling the first one Arthur.

'Well, Arthur, though young, was a post-war R.A.F. product, and quite a good pilot. He noticed the peculiarities of the "Iron Swine" as soon as he flew it—who wouldn't?—and had the sense to treat it with respect. As a matter of fact, he put in quite a number of flying hours with it, mostly taking parties of his pals on trips to the Continent.

'The "swine", finding that it couldn't disconcert him with its aerial antics, hit him on the head with its airscrew one day when he was "sucking in" prior to starting the engine and that was the end of Arthur. The Air Ministry held the usual enquiry, .and found that the switch was definitely off at the time of the accident, and that there was no apparent defect in the ignition system. The "swine" had miraculously produced a spark out of thin air in just one of its cylinders, and this had sufficed.

'As a precautionary measure, the whole system was re-wired, and the machine was purchased from Arthur's executors by owner number two, whom we'll call Bill, and this is where most of you will identify the "iron swine", because Bill fitted it up with special tanks to fly the Atlantic, and it got him across! The only snag was that he lost his bearings in fog, and finished up in the Swiss Alps, upside down in a snowdrift. The drift was a good twelve feet deep, and the "swine" was hardly damaged except for broken propeller and rudder; but it trapped Bill, and he was found a week later, starved and frozen in.'

'Why,' broke in Ralston—a very junior member—'that must have been—' But Beckett stopped him there.

' "No names, no pack-drill",' he reminded him gently, and proceeded with the story.

'Bill's father,' he continued, 'sold it to a man who shall be named Charlie, and it was during his turn of ownership that I had to fly it. He put it into commission, you see, for taxi-work, and asked me to run it on a profit-sharing basis, as I had a 'B' licence, and he hadn't. I'd never been up in it before, and, for the first few landings, it had me guessing. However, I soon got it more or less "buttoned up", and did quite an amount of charter work with it, over a period of six months. I always treated it, though, with the greatest—er, well, not respect— who could respect a mechanical pig?—but caution and determination. Its previous history had made me think, and the very feel of it, as soon as I got into the cockpit, told me as plainly as the voice of Conscience it was a killer. At the same time I got a distinct impression that it had no suicidal tendencies, and so realised that I was fairly safe as far as actual crashes were concerned, provided I maintained my attitude of extreme watchfulness. One measure which I always took was to strap myself in—a thing I don't usually trouble about, except for aerobatics.

'Now, I suppose most of you blokes will admit that I've flown years enough to know something about it, and also that my sensitive imagination has not yet destroyed my flying nerve. If you don't, I don't give two hoots, hut an appreciation of the point will assist belief in what I'm going to tell you next.

'No doubt most of you who've done much flying have had those "jumpy" hours after a forced landing when you keep on thinking the engine has developed a "new noise". I've had the feeling myself, and learned to control it, but, as surely as I'm sitting here, the "iron swine" *did* make noises at me!

'This happened mainly when I was flying back "light" after a taxi job, and there were no passengers to hear. If I opened the engine flat out, it bellowed with rage—a sort of superimposed bellow, entirely distinct from the normal sequence of mechanical sounds. When I throttled back a bit, the whole aircraft *snarled* at me, and, at really low "revs" and cruising speed it would squeal like the dirty sow that it is.

'The outfit, for the benefit of any of you who have *not* got it taped, is a low-wing monoplane with a humped back, and the pilot's accommodation consists of a double cockpit fitted out with side-by-side dual control, so that two pilots can collaborate on a flight, either one taking over on a course if the other wishes to retire into the passenger saloon for a rest. This saloon is, of course, completely enclosed and fitted with windows to give its occupants a view of the underlying scenery; but the pilot's compartment—situated forward, and immediately behind the engine —is only half canopied, having a bridge-piece in the centre, and two sizable apertures above, through which one can step from the wing into either port or starboard seat. Large as these openings are, the sprawling proportions of the machine dwarf them when viewed from a distance, and they take on the appearance of little, swinish, vindictive eyes peering cunningly over a blunt, gross snout. Sometimes when I had the "iron swine" parked at its base, at one of the London airports, I would go over to the hangars at dusk, and deliberately look it over as it stood in semi-obscurity, sullenly crouching its deformed, misbegotten shape in a dusky corner. It couldn't work miracles, much as it may have wished, but, without the bestial noises it made in flight, the malignant personality of the thing still cloaked it, and I could sense its aura of cold, relentless, controlled fury as it tried to weigh me up and discover a means whereby, despite my caution, it could kill.

'You fellows may think I'm shooting one hell of a line about a perfectly everyday mechanical contrivance which, ably controlled, could be made to show the precise, dynamic performance worked out on paper by its designer but I'm telling you that your guess is a joke. That flying monstrosity has the heart of a beast, and the mark of the beast stands out like a red scar in every line of its structure. If I were not a compassionate man, I'd like to pick on every pilot who privately laughs at my opinion and make him do ten hours solo on the hellion. It wouldn't bump him off by spinning into the deck. Good Lord, no! It's much too anxious to keep the inspired individuality with which its designer or craftsman has endowed it.

'Well, to get back to the history of this alleged aeroplane, there came a day when there were no contracts demanding immediate attention, and Charlie's garage business was slack. He came down to my hang-out, and suggested taking up the "iron swine" for a pleasure cruise to keep his hand in at flying. He had never taken the thing up solo, and didn't intend to on this occasion, but he'd flown it now and then with me in the spare cockpit, and had its idiosyncrasies more or less "taped".

'The perishing hulk was enough trouble to me on commercial work, without my wishing to fly it for fun, but, after all, he was the owner, and for various obvious reasons I could hardly argue the point.

'As I've already told you, I'd contracted the habit of strapping myself well and truly into the seat with my shoulder harness—and on that day I'm damn glad I did, for it was as "bumpy" as sin. Charlie, on the contrary, thought himself a bit above that kind of precaution. He had sense enough to realise that the "swine" was not a stuntable aircraft, but considered that, for straight flying, harnessing was a bit "old maidish".

134

'I let him please himself, probably against my better judgment, and proceeded to take off.

'Our—or rather Charlie's—idea was to fly down to Shoreham, do a matinee or anything else complying with our inclinations at Brighton, and trickle quietly back to Town towards sunset. He picked a "wizard" day for the trip—fifty mile an hour head-wind, and occasional gusts enough to lift you off the deck after you'd landed. I climbed up to a couple of thousand before handing over to C. I'm not so fond of inexperienced pilots pushing me about the firmament at no feet in that class of weather. Then I let him take over, and all went well till we got somewhere near Leatherhead, except for being thrown all over the sky by eddies and things several times per minute.

'In the mid-Surrey district the bumps became a thousand times worse—probably on account of the hills—and all of a sudden we hit the worst "sinker" I've ever struck. The "swine" fell out of Charlie's hands like a wagon-load of rubble, and lost about four hundred feet in the whisker of a second. Revelling as it did in that sort of emergency, it performed a couple of its own particular twitches, nearly cracking my harness, and shot poor old Charlie slap through the top of the cockpit. I didn't even see him go, having, as you can imagine, fastened on to the controls pretty swiftly. I'd heard the old tall story about an observer falling out of his 'plane during the War and being caught by his pilot on a power dive, but had as little belief in the yarn as I have now. Nevertheless, I thought I'd have a crack at it, and forced the "swine" into a vertical left-hand turn, with the nose well down. I caught another peach of a bump on the way round, and the "swine" put up another wriggle which damn near had me on my back, but I never even glimpsed Charlie's body as he dropped. He'd no 'chute, of course, and I knew he was a "goner", but as there was no field within

135

miles where I could have got down without crashing I headed back for London, where they'd already got telephonic news of the fatality.

'The "iron swine", having temporarily satisfied its blood lust, behaved wonderfully well for a change, and even seemed to carve up the air pockets disdainfully, on a dead even keel. It snarled at me a bit *en route*, but the noise struck me as representing the triumphant, though defensive articulation of a jungle animal poised over its "kill". It lacked the customary deadly antagonism.

'Charlie was married, and his wife had the settling up of his estate. One is glad to reflect that he left her well provided for. She hated all aircraft, and attended to the sale and disposal of his other assets before worrying about his cabin monoplane. Incidentally, I went on flying it for hire for some months, and handing her the profits, which were not inconsiderable. The thing was advertised for sale in the various aeronautical journals, but nobody seemed to want it, even at scrap price. It had gained a reputation for being "unlucky".

'The damn thing had several goes at me in the interim. Once it tried the original dodge of swiping me with its airscrew when the switch was off, once it jumped the chocks and made straight for me when a ground engineer was running up the engine, and on a third occasion it attempted to throw me out in mid-air, as it had with Charlie. Maybe it thought it could land itself without a pilot. I'd give it credit for even that ingenuity. In each case, fortunately, I was ready, and finally I got the credit of being the only pilot to fly a hundred hours on it without mishap.

'This fact, I suppose, pushed its selling-price up a hit, and it was at last bought by a fourth person who, for narrative purposes, shall bear the name Derek. He got it remarkably cheaply, and was highly delighted with his bargain.

'He was a fellow who'd done five years in the Service and a fairish bit of civil flying too, but he'd heard of the "iron swine's" freakishness, and got me to give him a landing or two before he took it up alone. I put him wise to its principal snags with regard to approaches and landings, and he seemed to get the hang of it astonishingly quickly. After twenty minutes or so he decided to go up solo for about an hour, and, on landing, confounded me by saying he *liked* the kite. Every other pilot I know who's flown it loathes the sight of the thing.

'I concluded that it had, for once, found a man it could take a fancy to, and that it might, in future, be quite a good tractable "flying pig". Had I paused to consider, I might have realised that its malign intelligence embraced no mean degree of subtlety.

'I got another contract about then, ferrying mails between London and Lisbon, and on the expiry of this found Derek all set for an attempt on the Cape Town record. He wanted me to join him as co-pilot, so that we could make a non-stop effort, taking it in turns to sleep; but I figured that, although the "swine" might have cottoned on to *him*, it quite definitely disliked *me*, and, knowing something of the route, I appreciated some of its unique opportunities of getting its own back on the only pilot who had consistently held it down. I accordingly made plausible excuses and left him to carry on with a promising young ex-sergeant pilot whom he had met—incidentally an accomplished navigator—just the man for that class of work.

'About a month ago, and some few days before they were due to start, I happened to be on Lympne Aerodrome, which they had chosen as their jumping-off point, and saw them warming up the engine for a test. The sergeant had done the "sucking in" with Derek in the cockpit attending to the switches. As soon as the engine got going, Derek climbed out of the "iron swine" and left it ticking over with the usual chocks before the wheels to prevent it moving. He busied himself rolling up the engine covers and screw pickets which had been dumped some ten yards in front of the machine, and his co-pilot walked over to ask me for a match. We stood talking for a few moments, and it was by the merest chance that I noticed, out of the corner of my eye something unusual in the behaviour of the "iron swine". Whether its engine revs. accelerated slightly, causing my trained ears to catch the sound first, I am not prepared to say, but when I looked straight at it, the thing was gently swinging its tail as though alternately operating its left and right wheel brakes, and, in so doing, *pushing the chocks aside.*

'Strictly speaking, it is a bad practice to leave an engine running without some responsible person at the controls, but I'm afraid I've seen it done very often, though I have never previously known an aircraft to move when throttled down. This thing, however, was accomplishing the feat, and I had never sensed a more diabolical threat than I read in the small, piggy eyes that were its twin cockpits. As it lurched free of the chocks and rolled forward at the unwitting Derek, I yelled a warning to him and jumped for the port wing. It nearly had both of us then, for, as if again automatically working its brakes, it swung fast after him as he ran, and would have damn near beheaded me with its trailing edge if I hadn't thrown myself down. The sergeant pilot—a devilish athletic man—cleared me in a jump, was up the wing to the cockpit and switched off the ignition.

'I heard the thing squeal at him as he did it.

'Well, it was no use talking either to him or Derek about an aeroplane possessed of a devil. They just hadn't the mentalities to picture such a thing, and put the whole affair down to a fluky sort of accident probably due to the fact that the grass was wet. I wished them a successful trip, and caught a coach for Town.

'The rest of their attempt is very recent history, and you must all know the main facts, though perhaps I can supply details not published in the Press, having had one or two private cablegrams from Derek, despatched at points *en route*. Apparently they got down to the Mediterranean without any particular trouble, and then the fun started.

'I fancy the "iron swine" was accustomed to Europe, and didn't like being taken South. At all events, they had all imaginable snags from engine failure to sand-storms, and lost all chance for the record in the first three days. After that, as you're aware, they kicked off to fly the Sahara and went missing!'

Beckett stopped, and moodily tapped his teeth with a pencil. In view of his gift for narrative, the yarn seemed strangely incomplete, and we all kept our mouths closed, wondering if he had anything to add.

At last the vicar broke the silence. 'I think you said earlier on,' he remarked, 'that you knew of five owners of this machine, but you have only mentioned four. Who was the fifth?'

Beckett looked at him with a very thoughtful expression.

'I am,' he replied unexpectedly. 'Derek and I were old friends, and he left the aircraft to me in his will.'

'But,' I interrupted, 'as the thing's missing and probably crashed, you can scarcely claim—'

Beckett transferred his gaze to me, and he is the kind of man who can stop the average speaker by that gesture alone.

'It hasn't crashed,' he answered. 'I received a cable from Cairo just before I reached the Club, telling me that it has been found in the desert by an R.A.F. rescue formation, nearly three hundred miles off its course. They were both good navigators, and I can only assume that the "iron swine" managed to fake its compass for them. It is evident that they ran out of petrol, and attempted to get away overland without adequate provisions, as their bodies have been located several miles from the aircraft and, of course, picked clean by vultures.'

'Well,' said Jacobs, the Club instructor, who had been a silent, if incredulous, listener, 'now the machine's yours, what do you propose to do with it?'

Beckett thrust out his jaw, and a hard light came into his eyes as he turned to his questioner. 'I've never done a parachute drop yet,' he observed with deliberation, 'and I wouldn't start 'em for fun at this stage of my career—but I'm going out to Egypt, and I'm taking a caravan to the "iron swine". When I reach it, I shall put on a 'chute and pour enough into the tanks to take me to five thousand feet. At about that height I shall tie the controls, step out, and pull the rip-cord.'

ANIMATE IN DEATH

W HEN EYSTON'S old schoolfellow, Raymond Cary, wrote asking him to spend a long fishing holiday on his newly constructed houseboat in Norfolk, the middle-aged journalist accepted the invitation with alacrity, little dreaming what lay behind it.

True, mid-winter did not seem the most attractive season in which to pursue this sport, but it was unquestionably the best time of the year for pike, and, from what he knew of Cary, he could trust him to supply alternative amusements when the weather proved really foul. Eyston was, moreover, a widower without family ties and, by vocation, strictly a freelance writer—both of which factors left him every liberty in the matter of changing his address. His only serious hobby was psychic research, and it was said of him by the very few who could call themselves intimate acquaintances that his real existence was bound up in this pursuit, and that his impecunious spasmodic reporting activities were an irksome interference that he only tolerated through sheer financial need.

He consulted time-tables, and wired Cary his hour of arrival at Yarmouth. The latter met him at the station with a baby saloon, and they set off for the hinterland with Eyston's suit-cases piled on the back seat.

'Well,' said Cary conventionally enough, 'glad you could come, old boy. Brought any fishing tackle? Haven't got any? No matter. I've plenty of rods and lines, and think I can promise you some decent sport. Should *love* one of us to take a record fish if only this other matter wasn't so—Still, you've not heard of that *yet!*' Eyston pretended not to notice the strained, even frightened look in his eyes and the incoherence of his speech. His friend was clearly troubled over something—and to no small degree but he preferred not to press him.

'As a matter of fact,' said Cary at last, 'fishing isn't my only object in asking you down. I naturally remembered your old-time keenness for it, but I also recalled your interest in the—well, er—the Occult.' He glanced momentarily from the road ahead at his companion's face, but Eyston replied only by an inquiring cock of the eyebrow. They were neither of them loquacious men. 'It's like this, you see,' Cary continued; 'as you know, I'm a sort of natural-born gipsy, and a year or so ago it struck me what an ideal existence it would be to live on a houseboat in some really isolated spot, whenever one felt like a rest from the noise of cities and travel. Being, as you also know, something of an all-round handy-man, I thought half the fun would be in making the thing myself. I did so in the yard of a local boat-builder— flatter myself I did it well, too—and had it towed by him to its present anchorage. The point is, I constructed every blessed bit of it, furniture and all, out of new timber, and it has only been completed a fortnight. It *can't* be haunted!'

Eyston lowered the near side window to throw out a cigarette stub, and methodically raised it again before offering any comment.

'But what makes you think it is?'

His friend drew in to the bank as the klaxon of an approaching car sounded beyond a bend; but the movement was mechanical. His eyes appeared to be focused on vacancy.

'A dream, I suppose,' he answered in a far-off voice, 'and yet a dream that was *real*. Oh, I don't know! Explain better when we get there.' He shrugged himself back into normality and accelerated. They crossed a bridge, turned into a by-road, and arrived some twenty minutes later at one of the infrequent staithes, or public landing-stages, that serve shore-going parties during the pleasure-boat season, and occasional sugar-beet wherries in winter.

Cary ran the car into a deserted barn and got out, followed by Eyston. 'Keeping the old barrow here for the present,' he explained, 'and I don't even have to lock it up. There are few holiday-makers about now, and the locals in these parts are very honest. That's my dinghy,' he added, pointing to a small craft moored between two hay-boats alongside the barn.

Dusk was now falling, and beyond the boats Eyston could see the unruffled sweep of one of the larger Broads fading away into the gathering evening mist.

His host lifted the luggage from the car and dumped it on board the dinghy. 'Perhaps you'd like to row?' he suggested. 'It'll keep you warm, and as I know the way to the houseboat it will be quicker for me to steer.'

He dropped into the stern seat and picked up the rudder cords while Eyston untied the painter and pushed off with an oar.

'We go practically straight across,' Cary went on. 'It's about half an hour's pull, and there's just enough visibility to see the guide-posts. For really bad fog I'll have to get a pocket compass.'

Eyston nodded, watching the landing-stage gradually vanish as he pulled out on the open water.

'The setting is first rate for ghosts and bogies,' he remarked. 'Suppose you tell me some more of what's on your mind?' His friend, eyes fixed on an approaching guide-post, hesitated for a moment.

'Have you ever dreamt identically the same thing two or three times?' he countered.

'No,' said Eyston, 'but I've met people who claim they have. Most occultists put it down to subconscious memory of an episode in a past life.'

Cary grunted. 'Yes, I know—but this isn't a memory. Look here, old man. I guess I'll leave you to experiment with the dream part of it at first hand. There is, though, a story concerning this water, which I *will* tell you now, because I honestly believe the two things are connected.

'Some time last July—I was at work on the houseboat then, and read of it in the local press—two girls were camping out on the Broads in a skiff fitted with an awning. They must have made a pretty comprehensive tour, for their craft—an unusual one in these parts— was noticed from time to time in various districts. They used to shift their location mostly at night or early morning to avoid the head wash and risk of collision occasioned by motor cruiser traffic which, as you may guess, is not always in expert hands.

'It was this habit which resulted in their arrival here somewhere between midnight and one a.m., and as it was too dark for them to find the staithe, and they were dead tired anyway, they tied up to the first reed-bed they struck and promptly turned in for the night. Possibly, in their haste, they didn't moor the skiff securely, for it was observed soon after dawn adrift in mid-water with the awning lowered. The staithe-keeper went out in a boat to rouse the occupants and bring them in shore, and found one girl fast asleep and the other missing. He naturally supposed the second girl had landed somewhere, until her half-awakened companion suddenly aroused herself, and asked him in some excitement where she was. The staithe-keeper suggested that she might have gone ashore in the night without awakening her, and that the boat had happened to break adrift at that particular period; but when, after a whole day's search, involving enquiries on all other craft moored in the vicinity, the missing girl failed to show up, it was taken for granted that she

144

had fallen overboard in her sleep, and caused the boat to come adrift.

'How this could have happened without the shipping of any water aboard the lightly balanced skiff and disturbing her friend, was by no means clear, but the other girl was so genuinely distressed that no suspicion of foul play on her part was entertained, and she was finally established at a local inn, having refused to remain on the skiff alone, while a more exhaustive search was organised.

'To make my ending brief, the missing girl never has been found, despite the use of drag-nets and the voluntary help of hundreds of holiday-makers who swam over the entire Broad, exploring the bottom as they went—an easy matter, as the depth is only four or five feet.'

Eyston rowed on in silence for several minutes. In any discussion of this nature he always tried to maintain an attitude of impartial receptiveness, as from experience he had found that too many queries and promptings sometimes suggested ideas to the other person's mind and confused his statement of facts.

He observed finally, when it became obvious that Cary did not mean to continue, 'I used to know all this water pretty well, and, to my recollection, the mud is both soft and deep. That could easily account for not recovering a body.'

'Mud be damned!' was the irritable reply, followed by a contrite apology. 'Sorry, old boy! Rude of me! But you don't know what I've been through! Four times in ten days—every time I've slept in that top bunk—the corpse thing has been my night-long companion—a hideously decayed yet living body—gesturing to me—supplicating—swimming!'

'Steady,' warned Eyston as they ploughed on through the darkening mist, 'if this show is jarring your nerves like that you'd best quit. In the meantime you've got me interested and I want to smell around.

We can stay up all night if you like. I suppose you've got some food and beer on board?'

'And so, you see,' Cary ended up, sipping his eighth Scotch and splash, 'the thing finally got beyond me, and you were the only consultant I could think of. I've had no previous experience of such matters, and I'll admit candidly that I'm scared stiff. It's not only the ghastly aspect of this rotting carcass, but the terror of *knowing* I'm asleep and yet being unable to wake up.

'The first time *that* only seemed to last a minute or two—bad enough even so—but I *did* manage to force my eyes open at last, and came to my senses literally soaked in sweat. The second and third occasions were a bit worse. I kept closing my eyes, willing myself awake, and then opening them to find myself still hanging suspended in that veil of greenish water, staring at the writhing, worm-eaten body. The night before last was the worst of all. I *could not* awake! I tried—Oh, my God, Eyston—so hard! I even bit my fingers till they bled... *There* are the scars—real physical scars on my real, physical body. I remembered the exact conditions of falling asleep, precisely how I had been lying and how the furniture had looked in the light of the lamp which I had left burning; but, try as I would, I *could not* think myself back into reality. All that I saw *was* real: the green, cloudy water, the corpse, and the sluggish fishes. My ordinary life was cut off from me by an invisible, impalpable barrier, suggesting that Death itself had overtaken me. It was not until the body's rotting lips opened as though to speak and an eel swam out that I awoke out of that horrible sleep. I fainted then for the first time in my life—or, if you like, dreamed that I fainted—and came to lying just where your chair is on the cabin floor. Thank God it was then daylight! This is the first time I've been back since. I wrote you at once and stayed last night in Yarmouth.'

Eyston removed his pipe, and tapped his teeth thoughtfully with the stem, his features grave.

'The exact conditions you've described,' he said soberly, 'are quite new to me, but, by a sort of intuition that often helps me, I've a hazy idea of their cause. As far as you're concerned, in fact, I feel I can already give you *some* advice without going further into the matter.

'Your observation in the car was correct. Your brand new houseboat *can't* be haunted. It's the site where you're moored that *is*. Shift the houseboat and it's a safe bet you won't be troubled again.'

Cary broke out feverishly: 'But, Eyston, you don't understand! She—it—never actually *spoke*, but I could sense each time that there was life there—somehow imprisoned—trying to escape. The pity of it almost equalled the horror. Somehow I feel as if I had been positively sent here to be of some help. Of course, I know I can't do anything, being a hopeless ignoramus in such affairs. That's why I sent for you.

'You see,' he continued after a frowning pause, 'I've heard of such things as earth-bound spirits, even though I *haven't* believed. I'm convinced that this is one, and I *can't* shift the houseboat until her spirit is free. Also—why, I don't know—I've a conviction that it isn't the girl's own fault. She is the victim of either an accident or a trap set by devils. God knows just where her physical body really is—but I'm sure she's tied to it—snared as I was nearly snared two nights ago. She cannot die until she wakes, nor wake until she dies, but the *life* is there, the movement—unmistakably. It *isn't* just the water currents. Sleep in that bunk, Eyston, and prove it for yourself.'

The occultist shook his head and slowly poured himself out a glass of ale.

'No, laddie,' he replied firmly, 'I shall *not* sleep there. You yourself seem to realise the exceedingly narrow escape you have had by doing just that thing, and, for a man who hasn't studied spiritualism, your summing up just now was astounding.

'Probably,' he went on dreamily, 'it is on account of sleeping here. Your "subconscious" knows all about it. What I *will* do'—he straightened up in his chair—'is this. We'll clear off now in the dinghy, motor to the nearest 'pub' and stay the night. Tomorrow—I won't promise, but I *think*—we may perhaps settle the business.'

Cary demurred at first, insisting that they should pass the night in the houseboat, taking alternate watches, pleading for a séance to attempt communication with the missing girl, almost accusing his friend of cowardice. But Eyston was obdurate.

'Natural sleep or mediumistic trance would be equally dangerous,' he affirmed, 'if indulged in at this precise spot. How do you suppose the girl disappeared in the first place?' Then, at his host's mystified stare, 'Never mind that now. Call it a dimensional overlap—and trust me till tomorrow.'

It was nearly two hours later before Eyston succeeded in shaking off the importunate Cary, and finally reaching the sanctuary of his bedroom at one of the waterside inns. There, having locked the door, he moved over to the window and stood for some minutes gazing into the misty gloom.

'It's queer,' he mused aloud, 'how the man in the street always regards an occultist as a sort of case-hardened miracle-man. He is expected to go out into the most horror-haunted regions and hobnob with the Powers of Darkness as though they were a bunch of lawyers' clerks... Animated corpses, indeed! Fish-mangled, posturing cadavers! Ugh! Beastly! *And* I'm expected to sleep on that infernal houseboat where even a materialist like Raymond maintains he can't wake up... Still'—his voice grew sad—'if what he thinks is true, I suppose I must do what's in my power. Poor child! Poor child!'

He sat on the bed, slipped on to his right index-finger a ring of peculiar design, and, closing his eyes, concentrated hard on visualising the houseboat's lighted interior. Gradually, painted as it were, on the lining of his eye-lids, the picture took form. There was the oblong trestle-legged table in the centre of the cabin, bearing the remains of their impromptu meal—a half-filled whisky bottle, a jug of beer, glasses, a plate of sandwiches. To the right a matchboard wall, relieved by a few quite good etchings, mounted with *passe-partout*. Opposite, the glass-panelled door giving access to the stairs leading up on deck. On the far side, the two built-in berths, the upper one still with its blankets in disarray as Cary had left them at the time of his fear-impelled exit.

Eyston stretched out a hand—the one bearing the strangely-wrought ring—and touched the table. It felt solid—real. He rapped on its surface, and the rough-cut deal responded with the sound of the knocks. The stone in his ring caught the light of the hanging lamp, and reflected it with a queer brownish glow, half lucent, half opaque.

Eyston seated himself in one of the thrust-back chairs and riveted his eyes on the ring, deliberately forcing from his mind all thoughts except his concentration upon it. The stone seemed to swell as surrounding objects grew less distinct until it occupied the entire range of his vision. He unconsciously lowered his head, bringing his eyes still closer to it. The stone began to change colour. It darkened, glowed again, and slowly turned from the brown opacity of dried blood to a shimmering milky green. The diaphanous luminescence of it spread about him, accompanied by a sensation of semi-tangibility that was neither wet nor dry, warm nor cold. He merged into it, hung floating in it with a novel buoyancy that kept him suspended, though unable to move about. The medium in which he thus hung was like water, in that it upheld him from sinking, yet it was not water, for it offered no resistance to the movement of his limbs, and so afforded no purchase to propel himself. Its stillness and utter silence were unreal, unworldly. He felt himself drugged to a state of arrested animation that was neither life nor death, but he remained fully, keenly, conscious.

A movement in the filmy half-light near him drew his eyes to a second figure sluggishly writhing at his side. He beheld the haunter of Raymond's dreams and thanked God that his friend's description had partly prepared him for it. He had seen dead men on battlefields, and the bodies of the long-drowned salvaged from the sea, and was thus inured to mutilation in the physical flesh; but, just as Cary had said, the frightfulness of this thing lay in its persistent hold upon life when, by medical standards, life must have been unthinkable for weeks, for months! The emaciated sodden legs beat a ceaseless march on the unresisting veil, like those of a gallows victim marking time in air. The battered, half-eaten arms clawed blindly at nothing. The eyes were gone, and within their ragged-edged hollows was manifest the coiling purposeful movement of reptilian life.

About rents in the tattered clothing that still hung upon the decayed body darted shoals of weirdly-shaped, unearthly fish—the only natural seeming things in that unholy realm. They circled the corroded face, tugging playfully at wispy strands of flesh as will minnows at an angler's bait.

Eyston, mastering the strong revulsion that held him, spoke and found that his words came audibly—even clearly—in the stillness.

'Tell me your dream,' he suggested gently, and turned his eyes resolutely away. A loathsome, bubbling groan answered him, and then, after a pause, a broken, distorted voice as the lungs strove to operate.

'Oh, God! Did—someone speak?'

'Yes, tell me your dream,' Eyston repeated, 'and lie quite still while you tell me, or you will make yourself worse.' His tones were soothing, caressing, like those of a bedside physician. 'You've been very ill, you know,' he added, then steeled himself for the burst of hysteria that followed, steeled himself against the gurgling articulation of organs that had no right to be exercised.

'*Lie* still!' said that awful voice. 'How can I *lie* when I always float upright with the fish and worms eating me—eating forever more and more away, till at last there shall be an end! Last week or was it last year? —they took my eyes, when I grew too tired to move the lids and so I frighten them. *Lie* still! When the flesh off my back is gone, and only the bared bones stand between my heart and the water. Look, if you can see. I am *not* dreaming. I *can feel—and* I know?'

The figure thrust a long-taloned hand among its shredded raiment and drew forth a writhing eel.

'That—*that* was *eating my stomach. Look* if you have eyes left to you. They have taken mine. I am blind, I tell you—*blind!*'

Eyston shuddered as though ice filled his spine. Never in his long and varied career had he met—or imagined—a haunting like this! And Cary, and the rest of them, expected him to treat such matters with the calm assurance of a skilled surgeon—brought him the cases which threatened their own sanity, and believed that, to him, they were just matter-of-fact happenings—that he could walk immune among things that the world could not comprehend, and of which he himself understood but the outside fringe. Why, in God's name, had he ever probed into ghostlore, and why, above all, had he ever made the fact public?... Still, sometimes people—and *things*—*needed* help... *This* thing, for instance, had it been man or woman when it was recognizable?—needed it ... he would do what he could.

He waited for the paroxysm to subside, and forced himself once more into the role of practitioner.

'You must be calm,' he insisted, 'or your recovery will be retarded. While your body is safe in hospital, your mind remains in some nightmare you have experienced. As for thinking that fish have eaten your eyes, it is simply part of your delusion. Your treatment requires us to keep you for the present in a dark room.' The positive assurance in his voice was not without effect upon the tormented, riddled corpse floating beside him.

'Thank you, Doctor. I—I believe you,' it managed with a hideous effort, 'and I will try to tell you—but oh! This horrible feeling of fish-es—inside me.'

'Never mind the fishes,' Eyston replied in soothing tones, marvel-ling at his own control of speech, as he watched the foul things swim past, mouthing the fragments of their meal.

'Well,' began the corpse, 'Florrie and I went to sleep on the skiff. Oh!'—interrupting itself—'Is she all right?'

'Certainly. She will be allowed to see you tomorrow,' lied Eyston.

'And then—I don't know how soon—I began to dream, and I thought I had stepped out of the boat, not into the rushes where we had moored, but up some worn, water-logged steps into a sort of empty house. There was a big central hall with sort of doorless wood-en archways leading off into different rooms, all very cobwebby, and quite empty of furniture. One archway opened on to a flight of stone steps leading down to still green water like a—a sort of Roman bath, you know?'

Eyston nodded before he remembered the futility of it. 'Yes?' he put in quietly.

'Well, it looked ever so attractive, and somehow I didn't think it would be cold, although it was all built inside the house and the sun couldn't have got at it—so I just walked down the steps. I was still wearing some of my clothes, but it didn't seem to matter in the dream. And then I jumped in and—it wasn't water at all, but this green stuff we're floating in now—' The voice rose shrilly, hysterically again.

'Remember I can't see it,' Eyston said sharply, and forgave himself this second lie as he uttered it.

'No! Oh, no. I'd forgotten that,' the voice replied in puzzled accents. 'Well, then, doctor, I suddenly realised that I must be dreaming and I naturally expected to wake up—but I just didn't—I *couldn't*. I tried ever so hard, and kept shutting my eyes and imagining the skiff with Florrie asleep at the other end, and then opening them once more. And all I could see was this green stuff, so I closed my eyes again and tried to feel for my electric torch—but all I could touch was fishes—wriggling.

'Then I thought I could get back the way I'd come, but somehow I couldn't find the steps. And then I found I couldn't move at all—at least I could move my limbs, but they didn't get me anywhere. I tried to swim and just hung suspended in this stuff that *isn't* water. I've been here ever since. It seems—oh!—years and *years*.

'First I got hungry and had nothing to eat, and then it was thirst— such *awful* thirst, and I tried to swallow the green stuff, but it did no good because it wasn't really liquid. I was *breathing* it, anyway! And then the fishes began on me—not all together at first, but singly, swimming by me and snapping at me as they passed.

'After a while they grew bolder and came for me in shoals. I tried

153

to beat them away with my hands, but they were too many. They came from all sides and bit and tore pieces out of my body. It was a long time before they ate any parts of my limbs because I kept moving them. And all the time I was trying to remember it was just a dream—that it *must* be a dream because I did not die. But it went on—and on—and on. 1 *couldn't* wake up! I *still* can't wake. Oh! doctor, open the shutters and let me look at the daylight again! Then I shall *see* my way back to wakefulness, and this horrible pool and the fishes will fade at last!'

'I cannot have the shutters drawn before tomorrow,' Eyston answered. 'You are undergoing very special pathological treatment which you would not understand. Now I must leave you for a little while, but first I want to place on your finger a ring. You won't be able to see it in the dark, but you can feel it; and I want you to concentrate all your attention on it until I come back. It will help, because it is something that comes from *outside* your dream. Try to ignore the fishes which seem to be attacking you, and think hard about the ring.'

While speaking, Eyston pressed a catch in the stone of his own ring, which at once divided itself laterally into two thin halves. The upper one he took off, and, conquering an overwhelming sensation of physical sickness, passed it over the flaccid forefinger of the corpse's right hand.

'Thank you, doctor,' came the gurgling voice, 'I will *try* to forget the fishes—Ugh!'

Eyston shivered afresh as he saw a snake-like head force wider the struggling lips. Then he closed his eyes and strove intently to visualise the details of his room at the inn, and particularly those of the open suitcase on his bed where reposed a *third* joint of the strange jewel.

Raymond Cary was in no very amiable mood on the following morning. He had, for one thing, taken too much whisky overnight and was irritable in spite of a dreamless sleep. He groused at the breakfast, the weather—for an annoying drizzle had now set in—and blamed Eyston for being a late riser.

'And now you've had time to deliberate,' he concluded, 'what *are* you going to do? I can't live on that houseboat as things stand, and I don't feel like moving it and leaving that poor, horrible, earthbound thing to its fate. *Can* you lay it or exorcise it—or whatever you people call the process—or must I call in the whole Psychic Research Society?'

Something in the grave regard he encountered quelled the outburst.

'Yes,' replied Eyston calmly, 'I *can* lay it, and in a more material practical manner than you probably expect. All I require is a powerful motor-launch with someone to operate it, a medium-sized dragnet, and your co-operation.'

'But,' Cary expostulated, 'the dragging's been done already! It's impossible they missed the body. Big as it is, the whole Broad was worked. It took 'em weeks!'

Eyston raised a commanding hand. 'You've asked my help,' he said authoritatively, 'now accept it in my way—and *don't raise objections*—or—'

'Sorry,' his friend returned. 'You win. The proprietor has a speed-boat. I'll see about getting it.'

The innkeeper, a youngish, retired fisherman, not without intelligence, was very willing to offer his boat and his own services as pilot when the intention of his two guests had been explained.

'Mind you, gentlemen,' was his immediate comment, 'I don't think we've the least chance of finding the girl's body after the search that's already been made, nor do I see the need to use two hundred horse-power for moving the houseboat, but, if we *don't* succeed, I'll only charge you the price of the petrol—and, if we *do*, why, I'll just feel proud to have helped.'

Eyston nodded his thanks. 'Good,' he returned with a smile. 'Then we'll start at once, and I want you to follow my directions closely. When we get there Mr. Cary and I will board the houseboat and secure it to your craft with towing hawsers. We shall then unlash it from its mooring-posts, and, in the meantime, you must keep your bows pointing to the open water and your engine idling. Watch me over your shoulder, and, as soon as you see my left hand go up, push your throttle wide open and keep flat out for about a hundred yards. You can then decelerate and stop in your own time.'

'Right, sir,' the landlord replied briefly, and led the way down to his private wharf.

A few minutes later they were roaring up the dyke at forty knots, twin waves a good eight feet high trailing like wings at the stern.

'There's one more job for you,' Eyston shouted in Cary's ear. 'When we go aboard I want you to take the dragnet and secure it aft of the houseboat while I'm fixing the towing cable to the opposite end. As soon as that's done give me the wire, and then hang on to the rail like grim death.'

At the speed of which the motorboat was capable it was not long before their destination hove in sight, and soon the owner had brought them skillfully alongside.

They vaulted to the houseboat's lower deck, and the preparations went forward as Eyston had planned.

His face looked worn and strained in the watery sunlight as he finally took his position in the cabin doorway awaiting Cary's signal that the dragnet was fixed. His right hand gripped a door-post with all the strength at his command, and Cary noticed, as he turned to give the all clear, two sections of his friend's peculiar ring gleaming on the tense, white forefinger.

'Now!' shouted Eyston, and flung up his free left hand.

Cary remembered to cling hard to the rail, but, even so, he was not fully prepared for the terrific jerk that followed the tightening of the hawsers. His abdomen was brought into violent contact with the steel bar, and for a few seconds he hung over it completely winded and more than half stunned. But, even in that instant of pain and confusion, above the roar of the speed-boat's engine, his ears seemed to catch the sound of two heavy thuds in the cabin behind him—the first loud and definite as if caused by the fall of a heavy man, the second ill-defined and somehow, he thought with a shiver, *squelchy*! 'Yes,' he whispered to himself as, still doubled up with pain, he slowly turned from the rail, 'it sounded like a sack of wet meal falling from—the *top bunk!*'

The innkeeper was now slowing his engine, and its exhaust died to a gentle purr. Cary staggered towards the open door and gasped out: 'Eyston! Are you all right?' But there was no response.

It was then that a nauseating stench of decay swept out of the cabin and seemed to strike him like a solid mass. Coming on top of the blow he had received, it was beyond his endurance. He was instantly and violently sick.

Presently, the landlord's voice from the now stationary speed-boat penetrated his dulled senses, and he dimly saw him jump the rail and hurry across the deck. He had fallen on hands and knees when the nausea attacked him, and he now rolled over on his back. His half-closed eyes took in an expression of amazed horror on the man's face as he halted by the open doorway, and he managed to articulate, 'Where's Eyston?'

'I'll look, sir,' the other replied shakily. 'Lie there till you feel better.' And he walked, with compressed lips, into the cabin. Coming out again after a very short interval and looking nearly as sick as he himself felt, Cary saw him lock the door and put the key in his pocket. He also noticed that he was carrying what looked like a letter.

'Mr. Eyston is dead,' he announced abruptly, 'seems to have fallen and broke his neck. No heartbeat. I found this in his hand. It's addressed to you.'

'I must go and make sure,' Cary answered, struggling to sit up. 'Old Eyston dead! I can't believe it.'

The speed-boat pilot gently but very firmly held him prostrate. 'That cabin's no place for you in your present shape', he said in an awed voice, 'at all events, read the letter first. It looks as if he'd expected something to go wrong.'

Cary took it with shaking fingers and slit the envelope.

'My dear old man,' (he read).

'In case you find me either knocked out or even possibly dead at the end of our experiment, read this first and act as I direct. In fuller explanation of the haunting that has troubled your sleep I will tell you that, by what some people are fond of calling a 'kink in space', the girl on the skiff was not drowned but *transferred* in her sleep to some phase of dimensions parallel to our own but imperceptible to us under normal conditions. It must have occurred through the pure accident of mooring her end of the skiff at the precise point where such a transference was possible. How the thing actually takes place I know no better than you. As you are aware, though, you very nearly shared the same fate, and one can only hope that no one else will be unlucky enough to sleep in future at that exact spot. Because the body no longer occupied its natural sphere the soul could not leave it, and you, after your own narrow escape, can well imagine the never-ending procession of horror to which that soul has been subjected. Last night I projected myself into that other world where the body was suspended and saw all that you described. I placed, however, upon a finger of the living corpse a portion of a ring originally found in an Egyptian sarcophagus and believed, according to hieroglyphs engraved upon it, to possess what I had best call inter-dimensional properties.

'The factor of speed in moving the sections which I am wearing away from the location of the 'kink' I feel to be essential, though dangerous to the wearer of the ring.

'I earnestly hope, and am persuaded to believe, that the result will be the dragging back of that other section into our own world, and, with it, the missing body. If this proves to be the case, and I am not in a fit state to deal with the situation, place the remains in the dragnet in order to simplify the explanation of their recovery.

'If this ends fatally for me, old fellow, try to console yourself with the knowledge that Fate assigned me inevitably to a very stern duty.

'Yours ever,

'B. EYSTON.'

Cary dropped the letter and lay gazing blankly upward for several minutes.

'Mr. Desmond,' he asked in a stronger voice, *what is in that cabin?*' The landlord swallowed and looked away evasively.

'Mr. Eyston, dead, as I told you,' he replied at last, 'and lying across him an almost fleshless body—pretty near a skeleton!' He shuddered and fell silent, while Cary slowly struggled into a sitting posture.

'You must have noticed that odd ring my friend was wearing,' he said thoughtfully. 'Did you happen to see if there was one like it on a finger of the—skeleton?' The landlord shook his head.

'There was no ring at all,' he affirmed huskily, 'but I must also tell you that the right forefinger of both Mr. Eyston and—the *other thing* are missing.' He hesitated once more, then added hurriedly, 'I've only once seen a man with a hand mauled like Mr. Eyston's. *His* finger had been torn out by a giant pike!'

THE AUTHOR'S TALE

'WELL, THE ONE I think I'll tell you didn't start off as a ghost-story at all,' said the well-known Author, putting down his glass. 'A "thriller", yes—a torture tale, in fact, after the best tradition of Poe—but something went wrong with the plot, and it finished up in the regions of the uncanny.'

'We agreed to stick to facts,' the Big Game Hunter reminded him, 'not the *plots* of dramatists.' The B.G.H. had been telling a few himself, mostly about African witchdoctors and Indian fakirs.

'Sure,' replied the Author, with one of his rare smiles. 'This is fact—only, as I meant to convey, it began as a human drama of revenge, and then the punishment was taken out of the avenger's hands by—*something else.*'

The rest of us drew our chairs nearer the fire. It was raining too hard to permit our customary Saturday 'foursome', but we were not inclined to start for our homes and get a soaking that way.

'Go ahead,' said the Barrister, producing cigars.

'Well, to begin with,' said the Author, 'the story concerns a bloke whom I used to know very well at one time, and whom, for want of a better name, we will call Lester.

'He was, I suppose, an ultra-rabid sentimentalist from the general standpoint. His profession doesn't matter, but his matrimonial ventures do. The fellow made a perfect habit of getting married—like a damn film-star. In fact, he was eventually nicknamed "Hollywood" by his closer associates. He was under twenty on the first occasion, and he got himself a wife who nagged. He found this out in a week or so, but as they lived in one small bed-sitting-room he couldn't get

161

away from it. She started mostly in the evening when he was tired after a day's work and wanted a spot of peace. After a bit he began to go pub-crawling to escape from the home atmosphere, and then she nagged at him for wasting his money. She used to have a go at him most mornings too, because he didn't have much appetite for the breakfast she had prepared. He stuck it for some years, being very young and rather of the Sir Galahad type. It just didn't occur to him that, having made marriage vows, he could possibly break them. Eventually, however, when the sex-appeal side of things had died a natural death, he realised that his initial idolisation of this woman—whose condescension in marrying him at all he had once considered goddess-like—had been converted into frank loathing. They had a culminating scene lasting the whole of one weekend, and she finally went back to her family. They were, fortunately for him, people of substance, and when she later on divorced him she didn't apply for alimony.

'Now, one might think that after an experience like that he would have devoted a few years to meditation before rushing into marriage again—but not a bit of it! Within a week of the *decree absolute* he was hitched up to a very snappy bit of work culled from a theatrical touring company, whom he had already been introducing to his friends as his "second wife" for some months. You'll notice that his Sir Galahad ideals were by now wearing a bit thin.

'Well, that show lasted for about a year—during which his finances failed to multiply—and then the lady poled off with another bloke possessing lots of "dough" and a yacht. Lester was very cut up about it because of the sensitiveness of his affections. He didn't mind about the other bloke—jealousy being absent in his make-up—and he quite saw the point about the yacht. But what he couldn't fathom was why she couldn't still go on loving *him*.

'Well, of course, everybody said this second fiasco would turn him into a misogynist—but did it hell! Inside of a year he appeared before the registrar with a third acquisition, and this time it really looked as if he'd backed a winner. The girl was quiet and unassuming, appeared completely devoted—even to the extent of taking off Lester's shoes and fetching his slippers when he came in—and was, after all, a damn good cook. Things went along splendidly for quite a while. She never nagged at him, was seen everywhere in his company, and couldn't do too much in the way of vetting his wardrobe. If you ever *did* meet him walking solo he bored you with her praises and declared he wouldn't part with her for all the money in Europe. This, mark you, after as long as three years! I should mention here that he had ultimate expectations from his family which she knew about, and, in the light of later events, this was probably what made her play up to him so cleverly.

'When he had saved a thousand quid by denying himself many of the pleasant things of life, he invested the lot in the purchase of a small business which he considered his wife—an erstwhile commercial secretary, by the by—quite capable of managing. His own work, by now, was taking him around the country a lot, and he left her in sole charge, going down to the place for weekends, but never bothering to audit the books.

'Now, beneath his wife's pose of affection, so long and carefully maintained, lay a mercenary and spiteful nature. The supposed paragon of virtue, who had *carte blanche* with the net profits, began to manipulate the turnover, feeling, doubtless, that Lester's "expectations" were overlong in materializing. In three months she ran up bills with suppliers to more than half the value of the stock-in-trade, and decamped with the whole of the liquid assets. He went home one Saturday to find the premises locked and deserted and, to be brief, had to sell out for a mere song, all of which went into squaring his creditors.

'Not content with this, she got a separation order on some trivial pretext of "unfaithfulness"—he had condoned several infidelities on her part—and tried to sting him for maintenance. The publicity of the proceedings lost him his job—so she was unlucky about that— but the treachery and ingratitude of the whole affair brought a hidden vein of violence through the crust of good nature which had previously enveloped him. He determined that she should pay. Not through any legal action for embezzlement. Oh, dear, no! He could not afford the costs and, in any ease, her sentence was likely to be inadequate by reason of her sex. She might, in fact, get away with it altogether. Lester was through with sentiment this time.

'Now, this is where the story becomes interesting. Lester, as I hope I have made clear, was naturally a forbearing soul. His first wife's nagging he had forgiven and forgotten almost as soon as it ceased; his second wife's desertion he had accepted with resignation. In neither case had he attempted to hit back. Now, however, his blood fairly boiled at the ingratitude with which his deeply emotional love had been rewarded, and he set methodically about nothing less than a reversion to Feudalism. He would kidnap this venomous swine of a woman and hold her captive in a secret place that he knew, flogging her daily until brute force brought her to absolute subjection.

'First, however, he had to live, and he borrowed two hundred pounds from his brother to keep him going until a job turned up. Then he made rather a long night journey to a certain destination, took a room at a village pub, and started his preparations. Before leaving, he had interviewed his wife and warned her of his intentions; but she had snapped her fingers at him, saying that such things just *couldn't* happen in the twentieth century. If he attempted to molest her she would obviously scream for help, et cetera. Lester smiled inwardly at this. It had not occurred to her that it would be necessary for her to make the journey in a drugged sleep on the floor of a closed car, nor that when she was released it would be under similar conditions and at a point far from the scene of her captivity. She might certainly relate her experiences, but that would amount only to her word against his, and he could bring crowds of witnesses to prove that he had never swatted anything bigger than flies.

'Two miles or so outside the village where Lester took up his abode was a derelict farmhouse standing quite alone in a hollow and surrounded by dense undergrowth. So ubiquitous, in fact, had the brambles now become that it was next to impossible to reach the ruin from any direction without suffering serious laceration. This made it peculiarly safe from the visits of unwanted "hikers", while the local rustics and their children gave it a wide berth on account of its reputation of being haunted.

'Lester was not particularly troubled about ghosts. As a boy, in any case, he had frequently explored the deserted homestead in search of birds' nests without encountering anything of an uncanny nature, despite the fact that his youthful imagination had made him susceptible to the possibilities latent in village gossip. It must be admitted, though, that he had never ventured near the farm after sundown.

'At the period of which I am speaking it is doubtful whether the place's evil reputation ever seriously crossed his mind. His chief interest lay in the fact that it was abandoned—isolated—and that in its seclusion he could work his will upon another human being with complete security from intrusion or interference.

'His early rambles had put him in possession of a secret which, to the best of his belief, was unshared by any other living person. Deep in the foundations of the building existed a spacious cellar whose only means of access was by a trapdoor flagstone hidden under a heap of rubble in the tumbledown kitchen-parlour. He had first discovered it during the "treasure-hunting" craze which attacks most schoolboys, but had been badly disappointed at the complete absence of "treasure". The floor of the cellar, reached by a winding flight of stone steps, lay some thirty feet below ground level, and though the youthful Lester had not found so much as a forgotten bottle of wine to reward his search, he had, for some unexplained reason, kept his discovery to himself—a course of action which now seemed to have been providential. With the flagstone dropped, the cellar would be most effectively soundproof. The most frantic human screams imaginable would fail to reach the ear of a possible (but unlikely) passerby.

'Lester's principal difficulty lay in importing the timber necessary for his purpose without exciting anyone's curiosity, but this he contrived to do under cover of night by stealing baulks of ash from a local timberyard, conveying them to the place in his car, and laboriously dragging them through the thorny wilderness that surrounded the ruin. He accomplished the task in one trip, leaving the wood stacked in a dilapidated outhouse, and carried it to the cellar on the following day.

'He next proceeded systematically with the construction of the device that he had in mind. It was to be an oblong frame, eight feet high by five feet wide, having a ratchet pulley gear at each corner so that a woman of average build could be mounted in it like a picture, her wrists and ankles held by straps attached to the pulleys. The latter could be operated to extend the hands and feet towards the corners of the frame, stretching the whole figure into the form of a letter "X", and restraining any attempted movement while corporal punishment was in progress. One short end of the rectangle was to be secured to the floor by substantial hinges, while the opposite end would be connected by ropes to two pulleys in the ceiling. Thus the mounted form could be raised to a vertical position for flogging, and lowered to the ground in order that it might subsequently be relaxed for periods of rest necessary to the continuance of health and ability to bear further punishment.

'Lester took the precaution of posing as a commercial traveller to account for his prolonged and irregular absences from the pub. He had previously purchased his hinges, pulleys, and screws from iron-mongers in various districts, .and had brought the requisite tools with him in his car.

'It took him four days to construct his apparatus, and towards the evening of the fourth day he was at work on the final touch—the overhead pulleys.

'On the previous days, so he told me, he had knocked off work no later than seven o'clock, though he could naturally have expedited the job by working well into the night. He had felt, however, a certain vague distaste for remaining on the premises at a late hour, and had even taken a small risk of discovery by leaving the flagstone raised all the time he was below-ground—this in spite of the fact that no daylight could reach the cellar at any hour, and that all his labours had had to be carried out by the illumination of a petrol lamp.

'Towards the conclusion of his task, the time being nearer eight than seven, the sensation of distaste had grown to a condition of acute uneasiness and, on descending from the shored-up frame, which he had used as a trestle for reaching the roof joists, he realised that his feelings amounted to fear. The walls seemed to be closing in against the feeble resistance of the lamp, and an inner voice kept repeating in his brain: "Get out, you fool—*out* before *they* arrive!"

'Lester, though, for all his sentiment and imagination, was no coward. Another detached part of his mind told him simultaneously that the disagreeable sensation was no stronger than usual; but that, before, he'd simply been too busy to notice it. He decided to stay and test the mechanism before returning to the outer air.

'The ropes from the top pulleys were tied to a staple in the opposite wall. He kicked away the supporting struts, untied the ropes, and lowered the frame to the horizontal.

'Yes, the pulleys were working freely, and would do so, he felt sure, when the frame carried its load. He stooped to inspect the adjustable corner thongs and, as he did so, saw, or imagined, in the tail of his eye, the flicker of something moving. His heart jumped to his mouth at the thought of discovery, and he jerked round towards the corner where the movement had appeared to be. There was nothing there—animate or otherwise—nor was there the slightest draught to cause shadow-dancing.

'"I'm getting nerves," he muttered, and resumed his inspection: thongs, plaited leather, strong enough to hold a gorilla—pulleys, oiled to silence, and working like roller-bearings—ratchets dropping into place without a fault to hold the thongs at any desired tension. Yes, the job was good... What the hell was that in the corner?

'He swung round again, and again saw nothing.

'"Too keyed up with the next move," said Lester aloud. "I must pull myself together or I shall slip up on getting her here." With slightly unsteady hands he lit a cigarette, inhaled deeply and sat back on a corner of the frame. As he did so a slim, white arm reached out and beckoned to him from a shadowed corner; though, of course, when he turned towards it there was no arm to be seen.

'Lester now appreciated that the place *was* haunted, but, curiously enough, with the realisation all sense of panic left him. He described himself as imbued solely with excited curiosity. What was this thing that moved and signalled to him when he looked away, yet vanished as soon as he tried to focus it? He concentrated upon keeping very still and trying to catch it off its guard by stealing half-glances at it from an averted eye. There it was again—a tall, white figure leaning against the wall on his extreme right, one slender arm extended and slowly waving a tapering hand in his direction. By an immense effort he managed to keep his gaze straight ahead, striving to take in as much detail as he could. The figure, hanging tantalisingly on the very fringe of his vision, seemed to be that of a nude woman, dark-haired and red-lipped, but with flesh of a horrible, unnatural pallor reminding him of the flaccid whiteness of dressed tripe.

'He shuddered, but, still keeping his eyes averted, edged himself a few feet away, hoping to entice her into the direct light of the lamp. Before he had time to test the success of his ruse he was shaken by a fleeting glimpse of a second white figure just visible in the corner of his other eye. He ripped out a startled oath, and involuntarily turned to face this new arrival. Nothing was visible but the bare stonework and the floor littered with wood-shavings; though he could have sworn to the existence of that second figure, deathly white as the first, but bearing the hirsute stamp of masculinity.

'Yet could he *swear* to the existence of either?

'Exercising tremendous self-control, he again riveted his attention on a blank piece of wall, and immediately became aware of white-limbed movement *on either side of him*. He rose to his feet and deliberately made a complete revolution, his eyes taking in the unrelieved bareness of each wall as he faced them in turn. But all the time white, weaving figures mocked the corners of his eyes. Good heavens! The cellar must he teeming with these things which he could only half see!

'He resolved to make a new test. Were these forma tangible? Once more, but closer now, a hand was beckoning on his extreme right. He reached sideways towards it, felt his fingers taken in a firm but ice-cold grip, and, resist as he would, *had* to turn his head. His hand retained the sensation of being clasped by another, but of this not even the outline was visible, though he could see white indentations of pressure upon his own fingers. He tried to snatch it away, but instantly another set of fingers closed upon his wrist, and he felt his palm drawn caressingly over the chill but pulsating contour of a woman's breast. Then wet lips, hot and passionate as the limbs were cold, pressed fiercely upon his own!

'Lester said afterwards that even curiosity left him after that burning salute. For all he cared the cellar might be peopled by a thousand ghosts. He felt the nude form that he could not see sink to the floor at his feet and draw him down beside her. A languid contentment filled him, and for a while he seems to have slept.

'A period of total oblivion was succeeded by one of half-conscious drowsing during which, lying with eyes half closed, he was aware of much agitated movement about the frame which he had built, and in the tail of his eye it looked as if several of the pallid creatures were grouped about it in attitudes of admiration, stroking it with their hands and making gleeful gestures. They seemed perfectly cognisant of its purpose, and were even testing it, tugging at the thongs and raising and lowering it by the ropes. Needless to say, as soon as he looked towards it they were gone, though the frame continued to move, while at the same moment there floated vaguely into the rim of his vision the white face and red lips of her who lay at his side. A soft, cold hand passed lightly across his forehead, lulling him, and again he relaxed into dreams. He dreamed of the woman whom he had loved last, and perhaps most deeply of all, who had requited him with greed and malice.

'Now, I think, in fairness to Lester, I should at this stage state my own belief that his intentions towards his wife were not only just but clean. He meant to keep her a prisoner in his frame, and to reason with her daily, patiently explaining her errors and emphasising them with a whip until he honestly believed she had learnt her lesson. Between the chastisements he would keep her warm with rugs, feed her properly, and even give her cigarettes—but the whip and sense of captivity were necessary, because in a state of freedom she simply *would not* respond either to reason or sentiment . Beyond the last his imagination had not travelled.

'He was brought back to remembrance of his present uncanny surroundings by the most hideous and prolonged scream his ears had ever known—a woman's scream of mingled agony and terror. Instantly his eyes were wide open, and he turned them automatically towards the frame, where the flicker of movement was now intensified. His brain in the same moment flashed him a warning that whatever was there would, as usual, vanish; but, to his amazement, this was not so.

'Strapped there, spreadeagled by the thongs, just as he had visualised his wife, hung the struggling figure of a girl, a torrent of cries— some full-throated, others choked as by some muted pressure— issuing from her mouth. Her clothing lay scattered upon the floor, and by the writhing of her body and incessant turning of her head this way and that it was plain that she was trying to resist the loathsome embraces of some real but invisible thing that hugged her. Soon her screams died to little moans and her terrified eyes closed, only to reopen filled with new despair, while her hapless struggles began afresh.

'Shouting hoarsely, Lester sprang to his feet heedless of unseen, restraining arms that sought to hold him down. He took one step in the direction of the frame and felt both arms pinioned in a vice-like grip, while the outer corner of each eye registered the presence of a tall, pale form sprinkled with tufts of coarse black hair. The girl in the frame seemed to realise his own presence for the first time, and called beseechingly: "*You* are human! Help me! Help—" Then something cut off her utterance, though he could see the lips, pinched in and distorted by some external force, striving to open. He essayed another step, but found himself helpless in his captors' grasp. "I can't move. They hold me!" he called back. Then a cold, sinewy hand sealed his own mouth. Abruptly he was flung down and held sitting, turned half away from the suspended girl; and once more, out of the tail of his eye, he could see the numerous weaving bodies that in turn possessed her and passed on into obscurity.

'Lester could never describe very clearly the after-events of that night. Alternatively he would sink back into a careless lethargy with the feeling of soft arms clasping him about, then find himself aroused by even more terrible screams and by gentle licking, sucking noises, indeterminate but very abhorrent. He held one recollection of seeing numberless wounds and rents in the skin of the captive from which blood welled. But the blood was never allowed to flow, being, it seemed, lapped up at its source by invisible tongues.

'There was another period of peace while kisses rained upon his face and a voice whispered to him of the evil, irredeemable soul of his wife, and how no punishment of man's devising could either uplift her or drive her back into the realms where she belonged. "Give her to us," murmured the voice. "She is our sister and will sport with us in our Half-Life—*after that humanity which she has abused has been taken from her."*

'Followed an interval of universal whisperings and rustlings broken now and again by the sound of crunching bones, gulps, and the unmistakable chewing of flesh, after which it seems that Lester fell into a dead faint.

'His next experience, with a return to full consciousness, was finding himself lying on the cracked paving of the disused kitchen, the early dawn twilight falling on him through the skeleton roof. For a few moments he rested there, wondering where he was, and—gradually realising that he was fully clothed and beneath open sky—thought that he must have had an accident with his car. Then remembrance flooded him and he sprang up in terror. The light of his lamp still glowed thinly beneath the raised flagstone, but it was many minutes before he dared approach the top of the steps. There he knelt and listened, but utter silence prevailed below.

'Half convinced that his nerves were to blame and that he had been the victim of an incredibly realistic nightmare, he finally steeled himself to the descent, and saw, with intense relief, that the frame was devoid of an occupant. Neither, thank God, were there any *stains* upon its woodwork. He leaned wearily against it and closed his eyes. This would never do! He had, supposedly, overworked, fallen asleep after finishing his task, and, cardinal error!—left the flagstone raised and the light on at an hour when the exterior darkness would show it up. If he was to effect the merited punishment for the accomplishment of which he had taken great pains, he *must* maintain his self-control. He opened his eyes again preparatory to turning off the light, and noticed, flung untidily into a far corner, a heap of woman's clothing!

'He was up the steps again like a hunted hare, pausing only to throw down the heavy flagstone before bolting for the place where his car was hidden.'

The speaker's voice lowered and ceased.

'And so,' I ventured, for a certain ring of sincerity had made the fantastic tale credible throughout, 'the project was abandoned perhaps, another prison chosen?'

The Author had relaxed in his chair, and his dreamy eyes seemed unaware of our presence. He replied distantly: 'On the contrary, I took her there the following evening and built a cairn over the flagstone to hold it down. Those things knew their job better than I.'

'You say *you* took her there!' the Barrister cut in with asperity.

'Did I?' said the Author carelessly, seeming to reawaken from a doze. 'Well, I suppose successful writers, like actors, must live in their parts.'

'B-b-but,' spluttered the B.G.H., 'we stipulated *true* ghost-stories!'

The Author laughed softly, indulgently, as he pressed the bell.

'Four bitters, steward,' he ordered.

Also available from
Shadow Publishing

Phantoms of Venice
Selected by David A. Sutton
ISBN 0-9539032-1-4

The Satyr's Head: Tales of Terror
Selected by David A. Sutton
ISBN 978-0-9539032-3-8

The Female of the Species And Other Terror Tales
By Richard Davis
ISBN 978-0-9539032-4-5

Frightfully Cosy And Mild Stories For Nervous Types
By Johnny Mains
ISBN 978-0-9539032-5-2

Horror! Under the Tombstone: Stories from the Deathly Realm
Selected by David A. Sutton
ISBN 978-0-9539032-6-9

The Whispering Horror
By Eddy C. Bertin
ISBN: 978-0-9539032-7-6

The Lurkers in the Abyss and Other Tales of Terror
By David A. Riley
ISBN: 978-0-9539032-9-0

Worse Things Than Spiders and Other Stories
By Samantha Lee
ISBN: 978-0-9539032-8-3

Tales of the Grotesque: A Collection of Uneasy Tales
By L. A. Lewis
ISBN: 978-0-9572962-0-6

Horror on the High Seas
Selected by David A. Sutton
ISBN 978-0-9572962-1-3

Creeping Crawlers
Edited by Allen Ashley
ISBN 978-0-9572962-2-0

Haunts of Horror
Edited by David A. Sutton
ISBN 978-0-9572962-3-7

Death After Death
By Edmund Glasby
ISBN 978-0-9572962-4-4

The Spirit of the Place & Other Strange Tales
By Elizabeth Walter
ISBN 978-0-9572962-5-1